AT THE BRAZILIAN'S COMMAND

BY
SUSAN STEPHENS

Published in Great Britain 2015
by Mills & Boon, an imprint of Harlequin (UK) Limited,
Eton House, 18-24 Paradise Road, Richmond, Surrey, TW9 1SR

© 2015 Susan Stephens

ISBN: 978-0-263-24856-2

Susan Stephens was a professional singer before meeting her husband on the Mediterranean island of Malta. In true Mills & Boon® Modern Romance™ style they met on Monday, became engaged on Friday and married three months later. Susan enjoys entertaining, travel and going to the theatre. To relax she reads, cooks and plays the piano, and when she's had enough of relaxing she throws herself off mountains on skis, or gallops through the countryside singing loudly.

Books by Susan Stephens

Mills & Boon® Modern Romance™

Master of the Desert
Italian Boss, Proud Miss Prim

Hot Brazilian Nights!

In the Brazilian's Debt

The Skavanga Diamonds

Diamond in the Desert
The Flaw in His Diamond
The Purest of Diamonds?
His Forbidden Diamond

The Acostas!

The Untamed Argentinian
The Shameless Life of Ruiz Acosta
The Argentinian's Solace
A Taste of the Untamed
The Man from Her Wayward Past
Taming the Last Acosta

**Visit the author profile page at
millsandboon.co.uk for more titles**

For the fabulous Ms M,
travelling companion extraordinaire

PROLOGUE

THE TERMS OF his grandfather's last will and testament had shocked everyone but Tiago Santos, to whom they had come as no surprise. To inherit he must marry. It was that simple. If he did not marry within a specific timeframe the ranch he loved in Brazil, and had built up into a world-class concern, would be handed over to a board of trustees who didn't know one end of a horse from the other.

His grandfather had suffered from delusions of grandeur, Tiago recalled as he prepared to land the jet he had piloted from Brazil to the wedding of his best friend, Chico, in Scotland. Tiago must give up his freedom to marry in order to preserve the Santos name, which his grandfather had believed was more important than the individuals who bore that name.

'The name Santos must not die out,' his grandfather had stated on his deathbed. 'It is time for you to find a wife, Tiago. If you don't provide an heir, our family will disappear without a trace.'

'And if I marry and we're not lucky enough to have a child?'

'You will adopt,' the old man had said, as if a child could be so easily co-opted into his plan. 'If you refuse me this you will lose everything you have worked so hard to rebuild.'

'And the families who have lived on Fazenda Santos for generations? Would you disinherit them too?'

'Your bleeding heart is wasted on me, Tiago. Do you think I care what happens when I'm dead? My legacy must live on. Don't look at me like that,' his grandfather had protested. 'Do you think I won this land with the milk of human kindness? What's so hard about what I'm asking you to do? You're with a different woman every week— pick one of them. You breed horses, don't you? Now I'm asking you to breed on a woman and get a child to bear our name. You know what will happen if you don't. You don't even have to keep her. Just keep the child.'

There was no way to argue with someone on his death-bed, and for that reason alone he had held his tongue. But one thing was sure: whatever it took, he would save the ranch.

CHAPTER ONE

THE FIST CAME out of nowhere and smacked her in the face. Flat on her back in the hay, reeling from shock and fighting off oblivion, she blanked for a moment and then fought like a demon. Cruel hands grabbed her wrists and pinned them above her head. Before she drew her next breath a powerful thigh was rammed between her legs. Terror clawed at her throat. Pain stabbed her body. The man was kneeling on top of her. She was alone in the stables, apart from the horses, and it was dark. The band at the wedding party was playing so loudly no one would hear her scream.

No way was she going to be raped. Not if she could help it, Danny determined.

Fear and fury gave her strength. But not enough!

She couldn't fight the man. He was too strong for her. Pressing her down with his weight, he was grunting as he freed himself, breathing heavily in anticipation of what he was going to do.

Yanking her head from side to side, she looked for something—anything—to beat him off with. If only she could free one hand—

He laughed as she strained furiously beneath him.

She knew that laugh.

Carlos Pintos!

Everything had happened in a matter of seconds, blinding her to all but the most primal sense of survival, or she would have recognised her brutal ex. It sickened her to know that Pintos must have tracked her down to this remote village in the Highlands of Scotland. Were there no lengths he wouldn't go to, to punish her for leaving him?

Coming here to Scotland, she'd been running home—running away from Pintos—running for her life. But no longer, Danny determined fiercely. She had escaped her brutal lover, and had no intention of giving way to him now. This was over.

As hate and fear collided inside her an anger so fierce it gave her renewed strength surged inside her. Bringing her knee up, she tried to catch him in the groin. But Pintos was too quick for her, and he laughed as he backhanded her across the face.

She recovered to find him braced on his forearms, preparing for his first lunge.

'Boring then—boring now,' Pintos sneered as a guttural sound of terror exploded from her throat. 'Why don't you admit you want me and give in?'

Never.

The only thing that made it through her frozen mind was that if 'boring' meant refusing the type of relationship Pinto had demanded, then, yes, she *was* boring.

'Well?' he sing-songed, sending her stomach into heaving spasms as he licked her face.

It had only been after she'd been going out with him for a while that Danny had discovered that Carlos Pintos, a big noise on the polo circuit, was a violent bully. He was always charming in public, and she had been guilty of falling under his spell, but he became increasingly vicious when they were alone. He must have used that same charm to get through security at the wedding.

Exclaiming with revulsion, she whipped her face away from his slavering tongue, knowing she had only one chance. With his weight advantage Pintos was over-confident, and he was taunting her by drawing this out. Gathering her remaining strength, she snapped up and rammed her head into his face.

With a yowl he reeled back, clutching his nose, blood pouring through his fingers. She lurched away, but the deep hay slowed her progress as she scuttled crab-like across the stable. Grabbing hold of the hay net on the wall, she hauled herself up and hit the bolt on the stable door. Barging through, head down, legs heavy and as weak as jelly, she lumbered forward, setting her sights on an exit that had never seemed further away.

Having escaped the wedding party, Tiago was taking a brisk stroll around the home fields of the vast High-land estate. As heir to a ranch in Brazil the size of a small country, casting a professional eye over farmland was second nature to him. His public face was that of an international polo player at the top of his game, but his private world was the wild pampas of Brazil, where he bred horses—a place where men were worthy of the name and women didn't simper. The press called him a playboy, but he much preferred being outside in a chal-lenging landscape like this to the cloying warmth of the crowded house.

Quickening his stride, he headed around the side of the house to the stables. His friend Chico had done well, marrying the heiress of this estate, though Chico had his own slice of Brazil to add to the pot, so it was a good mar-riage bargain all round. Chico intended to breed horses here as well as in Brazil—priceless ponies that might have been said to be the best in the world if Tiago's hadn't been better. He and Chico had often talked about expanding into the European market, and he could tell that this land had been primed and was ready for animals to raise their young in the spring.

Which was more than could be said for him, Tiago reflected dryly. Fulfilling his grandfather's demand that he find a wife was still a work in progress. He liked his freedom too much to settle down. The press referred to his Thunderbolts polo team as a pack of rampaging barbarians. He gave the tag new meaning—though the public liked to think of him rampaging with a glass of Krug in his hand and a beautiful woman on his arm.

He relaxed as he came closer to the stables, where he would be as happy chatting to a horse as making small talk in the ballroom. The courtyard in front of the block was dimly lit, in contrast to the chandeliers set party-bright inside the grand old house.

He was halfway across the yard when the door to the stable block burst open and a small female, dressed in some flouncy creation, tumbled out.

'What the—?'

Instead of reacting graciously as he ran to save her she screamed some obscenity at him and, grabbing hold of his lapels, roared at him like a tigress before angrily attempting to thrust him away. When this failed to make any impact she stepped back and, holding herself defensively, glared at him through furious eyes.

For a moment he didn't recognise her, but then…

'Danny?'

He knew the girl. She was the bride's best friend, and a bridesmaid at the wedding. He'd first met her at Chico's ranch in Brazil, where both the bride—Lizzie—and Danny had been studying horse-training under the heel of an acknowledged master of terrorising students: his friend and teammate Chico Fernandez.

'What has happened here?' he demanded as she continued to glare at him. She was panting as if she'd run a mile. Then he saw her face was badly bruised. '*Deus*, Danny!'

Moving past her, he stared into the darkened stable block. Nothing seemed to be out of place, so he turned back to her.

'Danny, it's Tiago from Brazil. Don't you recognise me? You're safe now.'

Battered and bruised she might be, but her eyes blazed at this last comment.

'Safe with *you*?' she derided.

Fair enough. If she believed his press, she probably should run for her life.

But she didn't run. Danny stayed to confront him. She'd always had guts, he remembered, and had never been afraid to take him on when they'd met at Chico's ranch. But what had happened here?

'Why are you out here on your own?' And where the hell was Security? he wondered, glancing around.

'What's it to you?' As she spoke she touched the red bruise on her cheek.

'Quiet, *chica*... You need help with this.'

'From *you*?' she demanded. And then she shrieked. 'Watch out!' and, giving him one hell of a push, she alerted him to the shadowy form looming behind them.

Shielding her with his body, he countered the attack and knocked the man out cold.

Carlos Pintos!

He loathed the man. Pintos gave polo a bad name. A cheat on the field of play, as well as in life, he was also Danny's ex—who had brutalised her, by all accounts, he remembered now. Toeing the inert figure with the tip of his boot, he reassured himself that Pintos wasn't going anywhere before calling Chico on his phone.

A few terse words later, he turned back to Danny.

'Don't,' she said, holding up her hands as if to ward him off.

They'd had many a run-in during Danny's time in Brazil, but theirs had always been a good-natured battleground, where he teased and she flirted. It had never gone any further than that.

'*Thank you* would suffice,' he commented mildly. 'And please let me assure you that I have absolutely no intention of touching you.'

He was assessing her injuries as he spoke. Judging them superficial, he considered the subject closed— though the police would have to be alerted, and he would wait until he was sure Pintos was safely under lock and key.

'Thank you,' Danny muttered, frowning as she stared up at him from beneath her eyelashes.

Straightening his suit jacket, he brushed his hair back and then asked bluntly, 'Did he touch you?'

'What do you think?'

'I can see the obvious bruises, but I think you know what I mean.'

Grimly, she shook her head. 'He didn't do what you're thinking. You men all think the same.'

She was upset, but he wouldn't stand for that. 'Don't tar me with the same brush as Pintos. And you still haven't told me why you're out here on your own.'

'I was in the stable block checking out the horses,' she explained grudgingly.

He didn't believe her for a minute. Chico had staff to do that, and even Danny wasn't so closely welded to her job.

'I've lived here all my life,' she murmured, 'and I've always felt safe here. Nothing like this has ever happened before. And if you must know,' she added, flashing a glance up at him, 'I wanted to be alone. I wanted to think...away from the noise of the party.'

'I can understand you wanting some quiet time,' he agreed—he'd felt the same. 'But times change, Danny.'

'Yes,' she said ruefully. 'Everything changes. But I'm still here.'

He guessed she would miss her friend Lizzie now she had married Chico, and perhaps Danny's scholarship to train horses in Brazil hadn't been the golden ticket she'd hoped for. 'It takes time to establish a career—especially a career with horses.'

'And money,' she said. 'Lots of money that I just don't have. And if there's one thing I've learned it's that I can't have everything in life.'

'You're wrong. Look at *me*.'

She smiled at his arrogance, but he knew that self-confidence was the first step towards building any successful career. If he hadn't believed in himself, who would have?

'It's possible for you to do this too,' he said, and when she started to argue, he added, 'I admit I was in the right place at the right time, but I worked all the hours under the sun for that luck—as you do. I always had a vision of what my future would hold. You have the same. So go for it, Danny,' he advised. 'Don't hold back.'

If there was one thing he couldn't tolerate it was bullies, and he hated seeing what Pintos had done to this woman—stripping away Danny's spirit and leaving only the doubt underneath. He found himself willing his strength into her.

He'd never been in this position with a woman before;

communicating with women on a serious level had never been necessary. His life was full of women, and he had never wanted this type of interaction with one of them. But to keep Danny steady after her ordeal, he continued on with his theme.

'When we first met on Chico's ranch in Brazil you wanted your own horse-training establishment. Am I right?'

'Yes,' she agreed, but she was shaking her head. 'I was idealistic then. I hadn't thought through all the pitfalls ahead of me.'

'And you think it's been easy for me?'

His face was close. Her scent bewitched him. He was pleased when her flickering gaze steadied on his, telling him she was calming down.

"I worked hard and never gave up my dream. And neither must you, Danny. Never...*never* give up your dream.'

Her gaze strayed to Pintos.

'Don't look at him. Look at me.'

He was relieved when she did so.

'Thank you.' Her eyes were wide and wounded. 'Thank you for reminding me what I want out of life, and that he has no part in it.'

'Don't thank me. You're strong. You'll get over this.' He glanced at the creep on the floor. 'He won't be bothering you again. I promise you that.'

'I'm all right—really,' she insisted, with a smile that didn't make it to her eyes.

She didn't want his pity. He could understand that. Danny wasn't the type to make a fuss. She didn't cry, or cling to him. She'd been one of the boys in Brazil, only caring for her horses and for her best friend—today's bride, Lizzie. She had always lifted everyone's spirits on Chico's ranch.

He glanced again at Pintos in disgust. The creep had been so eager to recapture Danny he had forgotten to do up his flies. 'I'll stay with you until Security arrives,' he reassured her, seeing she was still frightened of the man. 'I'll hand Pintos over to them and then I'll take you back to the house.'

'There's no need for that,' she insisted, shaking her head as she hugged herself defensively.

'There's every need,' he argued. 'You shouldn't be on your own tonight. And you should get checked over.'

She shook her head slowly, as if she were reliving events. 'I can't believe I let this happen.'

'You didn't *let* this happen, Danny,' he said firmly. 'You've done nothing wrong.'

She glanced at him then, as if seeking reassurance. 'Maybe I should take it as a sign that my time here's done.'

'Then don't stay,' he said with a shrug. 'But just promise me you won't make any hasty decisions while you're upset.'

'Upset?' she scoffed. 'I'm over it.'

He doubted that. 'Good, but please sleep on it, and see how you feel in the morning. Maybe you'll feel differently then.'

'Or maybe I'll think *Clean page, new story*.'

'That's also a possibility,' he conceded.

'But I can't run away,' she said softly, almost to herself. 'I can't run away from Carlos or from anything else.'

'You don't have to,' he reassured her. 'Change doesn't always involve running away. Think carefully before you make any life-changing decisions. And don't go wandering around on your own in the dark in future.'

'Why?' Her eyes cleared suddenly and she repaid him with a piercing look. 'Because you won't be around to save me?'

He met that stare and held it. 'That's right. I won't.'

Danny's feelings were in an uproar. Yes, she was shocked by what had happened in the stable, but standing next to Tiago Santos was incredible, and unreal, and incredibly unsettling even without having Carlos Pintos at her feet. She had been violently attracted to Tiago in Brazil. From the very first moment she had felt a connection between them, and it was still there.

Which only proved what a hopeless judge of men she was, Danny reflected. Tiago was a notorious playboy, and when they'd first met she had treated him as such— teasing him, yes, because that was in her nature, but keeping a safe distance from him, all the same. And now Tiago was handing out life advice. Was he the best person to do that?

Surprisingly, tonight she would say yes—because to-night he was talking to her as Lizzie would, and his con-cern for her appeared to be genuine.

'Security's here,' he announced as two guards ran up. 'We'll go back to the house as soon as we've spoken to the police.'

'I don't need a chaperon, Tiago,' she stressed.

'That's good, because I'm not for hire.'

'Why don't you go back to the party?' she suggested, having no inclination to jump from the frying pan into the fire. 'I feel really bad, keeping you here.'

'You're not keeping me,' he insisted. 'We'll go back together. I have to know you're safe.'

'How much harm do you think can come to me be-tween here and the front door?'

Tiago's answer was to stare at her in a way that told her he wouldn't be dissuaded, and in spite of his all too colourful reputation she had to admit she did feel safe with him. And she had to get over her schoolgirl crush fast, Danny cautioned herself. Tiago Santos was not for her.

'Just a few more minutes,' he said, staring at her with concern.

She smiled back at him, recognising that soothing, husky, faintly accented tone as the same voice he'd used to soothe his ponies in Brazil.

'You don't have to come back to the party, Danny. I'll make your excuses for you.'

'No, you won't,' she argued firmly.

Tiago raised a cynical brow over eyes that were dark and piercing. He was such a good-looking man it was impossible to remain immune to him. And he could read her like a book. He always had been able to.

The course she'd taken in Brazil had been so hard, and Tiago was a hugely successful polo international. She had always tried that little bit harder when he'd come to watch her working in the training ring. Her pride was holding her up now. He knew how shaken she was, but she didn't want him to think her weak.

As the seconds ticked by she longed for the sanctuary of her room. This situation was unreal, and she wanted nothing more than to strip off and stand beneath a shower, scrubbing every inch of her body clean. She had to get rid of Carlos's touch, and then hopefully forget she had ever been so stupid as to take up with a man like him in the first place.

She glanced at Tiago as he gave instructions to the security guards, thinking how different he was. Tiago's command of the situation was reassuring. He was every-thing the sorry excuse for a man at their feet was not.

Did the fates see any humour in the situation? she wondered. Tiago Santos, the world's most notorious play-boy, was no playboy but a protector—strong and caring. He might look dangerous, but his character was different from the way it was described in his press.

'Where do you think you're going?' he called after her as she started back to the house.

'We've spoken to the police. Pintos has gone—'

'I'm heading your way, remember?' he said, catch-ing up with her. 'Go straight up to your room and I'll tell Lizzie what's happened.'

'No, you won't. Lizzie's been upset enough tonight. She must have noticed I'm missing. She will have seen the lights of the police cars. This is her day, not mine. Let's not spoil it for her,' she said, desperate not to ruin Lizzie's day. 'Just tell her the fuss is over and there's nothing for her to worry about. Say I went to check on the horses and lost track of time. Tell her I tripped in the mud and had to clean myself up—I've gone upstairs to change my clothes and I'll be back at the party soon.'

'I'll do what I can,' Tiago promised. 'But I won't lie to her. Danny, you can't pretend nothing's happened,' he insisted when she scowled at him.

'That's not what I asked you to do. What?' she de-manded impatiently, when Tiago continued to stare at her.

A faint smile touched his mouth. 'You might not be able to keep it a secret.'

'Why not?'

'You won't win any beauty contests tonight.'

She touched her face and groaned, remembering the bruises. She'd forgotten about them.

'Do you have anything you can put on them?' Tiago asked with concern.

'I'm sure there'll be something in the house.'

'Maybe I should call a doctor for you?'

'A doctor won't come out at this time of night—and why would we trouble one? Thank you for your concern—seriously, Tiago—but it's only a bruise, and bruises fade.'

'And you don't have to be strong all the time,' he fired back.

'What's it to you?' Biting back tears, and hating herself for the weakness, she confronted him in the way they had squared up to each other on so many occasions on the ranch in Brazil.

It was a terrible mistake to stare into Tiago's eyes. Her awareness of him only grew. But she couldn't allow him to patronise or pity her, if only because it was so dangerous to wonder, even for a second, how it might feel to have a man like Tiago Santos care for her.

The first thing she had to do was get over tonight. Bruises would fade, but the disappointment she felt in herself for not progressing her career as she would have liked, for not moving away from her home town, and most of all for getting mixed up with a man like Carlos Pintos, would take a lot longer.

'I should thank you properly,' she said, remembering her manners belatedly. If nothing else, Tiago had been her saviour tonight.

He shrugged it off. 'No medals, Danny. They'd only spoil my suit.'

He could always make her smile. The playboy was still in him, beneath that white knight's shining armour. She must never allow herself to forget that Tiago Santos possessed a glittering charm that had led many women astray. She must never be guilty of romanticising that charm, because there was another man underneath it.

Brutal tattoos showed beneath the crisp white cuffs of Tiago's immaculate dress shirt, and a gold earring glinted in what light there was. This was not some safe, mild-mannered man—a white knight racing to rescue the damsel in distress—but Tiago Santos: the most infamous barbarian of them all.

CHAPTER TWO

ANNIE, THE HOUSEKEEPER at Rottingdean, was waiting for them at the front door.

'Chico told me what happened,' Danny heard Annie inform Tiago discreetly as the housekeeper ushered her away. She saw him nod briefly.

'Before you go,' he called after her. 'Here's my card. If you need anything...'

'Your *card*?' She smiled at the incongruity of a barbarian carrying a card, but took it and studied it before looking up. 'I won't need anything, but thank you again for tonight.'

Tiago ground his jaw. He wasn't used to being on the receiving end of a rain check, she guessed as he turned to rejoin the party.

She scrubbed down in the shower, turning her face up with relief to the cleansing stream. So what excuse did she have for being in the stables on her own at night, in the middle of Lizzie's wedding party?

She'd been having a moment, Danny concluded. She had needed some quiet time to contemplate her life going forward now her best friend was married. The stables was where she had always sought sanctuary, even as a child. The horses were so quiet and mild they had always been a relief—a release from her troubled home life—and tonight had seemed a good time for her to re-evaluate in that quiet place.

The last thing she had expected was for a nightmare like Carlos Pintos to reappear. Thankfully, he would be locked away for a very long time now. The police had told her this. It turned out he was a wanted man, who had stalked and attacked several women.

So all she had to worry about now was Tiago Santos.

Oh, good, Danny reflected wryly, wondering if she would ever get Tiago out of her head. While he was close by she could think of nothing else.

But where was she going with this? Shouldn't she toughen up and forget about men? Wasn't that safer? She would have to if she was ever going to give herself the chance of a career. And what was she waiting for as far as *that* was concerned? She had a prestigious diploma from Chico's training school in Brazil, as well as a lifetime of experience with horses. It was time to make that count. It was time to start planning for the day when she had her own equine establishment.

With an impatient laugh she turned the shower to ice. Maybe that would wash some sense into her. She was a few hundred thousand pounds short of the start-up cash for her own place, with very little prospect of getting hold of such huge amounts of money.

'Danny?' Annie was calling from behind the door.

'Yes?'

'There's someone here to see you, hen.'

The familiar Scottish endearment made Danny smile. 'Just give me a minute and I'll grab a towel—'

It would be Lizzie. She would play down what had happened. She would change the subject and make Lizzie laugh. It was her best friend's wedding day, when everything had to be perfect. And it would be if Danny had anything to do with it.

'I can tell him you'd rather not see anyone if you'd prefer that, hen?'

Him?

'He's very concerned about you...' Annie waited, and then, receiving no reply, added, 'I think you should at least see him to reassure him that you're okay...'

Danny's heart went crazy. She was actually trembling. There was only one man who knew what had happened in the stable. And she had just vowed to cut him out of her life.

'I've brought you a clean dress. I'll just leave it on the bed, shall I?' Annie suggested. A few more seconds passed and then the housekeeper called out with concern, 'Are you okay in there, Danny?'

'Yes. I'm fine.' She put her resolute face on. 'I'm just coming... Could you ask him to give me a few minutes?'

'Will do, hen.'

And now there was silence. Was Tiago standing outside the door, or had he gone downstairs to wait for her? She stood listening, naked and dripping water everywhere, with the towel hanging limply from her hand. Wasn't it better to face him, talk to him, reassure him as Annie had suggested? Then she could finally put an end to this horrible episode. Tiago must understand that she was very grateful to him but that she didn't need his help going forward.

Securing the towel tightly around her, she firmed her jaw.

She was keeping him waiting. No woman had ever kept him waiting before. He had to remind himself that tonight Danny was a special case. She'd had a shock and he was supposed to be playing the role of understanding friend. At least that was how the bride had described him when he had passed on Danny's message. Chico had already told Lizzie what had happened, so obviously the bride was full of concern for her friend.

'Be gentle with her, Tiago'.

What the hell do you think *I'm going to be with her?* he had thought.

'Just do this one thing for me,' Lizzie had begged him with her hand on his arm.

'I will,' he had promised, finding a smile to reassure the bride. And he'd kept his word.

In his hand there was nothing more threatening than horse liniment to speed up the healing of Danny's bruises. Was that gentlemanly enough?

Danny looked at the dress Annie had left on the bed with dismay. It was the type of dress she'd seen in magazines, but it was hardly appropriate for someone whose life revolved around horses. It was lovely, and maybe any other night she would have loved to try it on. If she was honest, she would love to wear it—but not tonight, when she was feeling about as confident as a cockroach with a foot hovering over it.

The dress was bright red silk, and the type of dress to get you noticed, darted in such a way that it showed off the figure. It was a perfect dress for a wedding party, for dancing, for having fun. It was Lizzie's dress. She recognised it immediately and smiled, thinking of her friend picking it out for her to wear.

So what was she going to do? Tiago was waiting outside. Lizzie was waiting downstairs. She didn't want Tiago thinking she was weak, and she didn't want to worry her friend.

She put on the dress and left her hair loose. Slipping her feet into Lizzie's silver sandals—they were almost the same size—she checked herself over in the mirror. She tipped her chin up and sighed. The bruises didn't look too bad now, but they were still noticeable even though she had covered them with make-up. But there would be atmospheric lighting downstairs for the dancing. No one would notice, she hoped. She was definitely going to pull this off.

He could hear Danny moving around inside the room. Why the hell didn't she open the door? He rested his head against the wall, and then pulled away again. He thought about walking straight in, and then remembered he was playing the role of a gentleman tonight.

'Nearly ready,' she called out brightly, as if the evening had held nothing more for her than a garden party and a chance meeting between old friends. 'Sorry to keep you waiting!'

I bet, he thought.

She swung the door wide and for once he was speechless. A transformation had been wrought and for a moment he wasn't sure he approved. He'd seen Danny in breeches and a shirt often enough as she sat astride a horse. He'd seen her in a fancy bridesmaid's dress, demure and contained—and then bedraggled, muddy and bruised later, which had brought out his protective instinct. But this red clinging number—far too short, far too revealing…

'You can't be thinking of going down to the party dressed like *that*?'

The words were out of his mouth before he could stop himself. The irony wasn't lost on him. Danny was dressed as he expected a woman on his arm to dress—but this was *Danny*.

And, seeing the way she was staring at him now, he braced himself for the backlash he knew was on its way.

'I most certainly *am* going down in this dress,' she told him, her gaze steely. 'It's all I've got to wear—other than a bathrobe. Or I could make Lizzie think I'm in a really bad way and upset her even more than I have already by staying up here in my room all night?'

He slanted a smile, guessing none of those options would appeal.

'If you'd rather not be seen with me—'

'I brought you this,' he interrupted.

'What is it?' she asked suspiciously, thrown as she stared at the tube he held in his hand.

'I use it on the horses when they get bruises. It works miracles.'

She angled her chin to give him an assessing stare. 'Does it smell?'

A muscle in his jaw flexed as she brought the tube to her nose. 'I must admit I hadn't thought about that.'

'Perhaps I should?' she said with the suggestion of a smile. 'For the sake of the other guests, if nothing else?'

He raised a brow, forced now to curb his own smile. Having taken in the hourglass figure, the glorious hair hanging loose almost to her waist, and the tiny feet with pink shell-like nails enclosed in a pair of high-heeled silver sandals, he was appreciating Danny's indomitable spirit as he never had before. The fact that she could be so together after such an ordeal was hugely to her credit.

'Thank you, Tiago,' she said briskly, before he could process these thoughts. 'It seems I have a lot to thank you for tonight. And I do...sincerely,' she added, holding his gaze steadily for a good few seconds.

It was time enough for his groin to tighten. 'You're certain you're all right now?' He had to remind himself that his thoughts where Danny was concerned weren't appropriate.

'I will be when I get back to the party,' she assured him, glancing at the door. 'I'm keen to get everything back to normal for Lizzie as soon as I can. I'll just leave this here, if that's all right with you?' She flashed him a glance as she put the cream down on the table. 'I'll put it on tonight, when there's no one else around to smell it.'

He was unreasonably glad to discover she would be on her own tonight. 'Shall we?' he said, offering his arm.

'Why not?' she replied walking past him.

She walked ahead of Tiago, and all the way down the stairs she felt the heat of his stare on her back. The fact that they were both so aware of each other was exciting, but also dangerous, and she had no intention of allowing Tiago Santos to see just how much his presence rattled her, or that the sight of him close up was all it took to unnerve her.

No man could achieve his level of success by being an angel, though she supposed he couldn't be held responsible for the way he looked—those eyes, that mouth, the way he stood, eased onto one hip, as if life were his to survey at his leisure.

She had lived in Brazil for quite some time while she was training at Chico's ranch, and she had come to love the Brazilian people for their warmth and exuberance. Tiago had those same qualities in abundance, though she had to remind herself of the rumours that said he was a lone wolf and dangerous.

It was almost a relief to be enveloped in the noise and

exuberance of the party downstairs, where she headed straight for the top table and Lizzie.

'Wow—you look amazing,' Lizzie exclaimed, standing up to greet her. 'I'm glad I picked that dress—it really suits you. Are you okay now?' Lizzie added in a quieter tone, and then she saw the bruises. 'Oh, Danny! Your poor face!'

'Is it an improvement?' Danny touched her cheek gingerly.

'Don't joke about it. It isn't funny,' Lizzie insisted. 'Pintos is a monster. Thank God he's locked away.'

'Let's not speak about him again, okay?' Danny put her arm around Lizzie's shoulder. 'I don't want anything to spoil your wedding day.'

Lizzie ignored the warning. They were both too stubborn to be curbed so easily, Danny supposed.

'I'm just so relieved that Tiago was there to save you,' Lizzie exclaimed, glancing round to look for the man in question. 'Maybe he's not as bad as they say?'

'He's every bit as bad,' Danny argued as she stared at Tiago, who was talking to the groom.

'I can't imagine how Pintos crashed the wedding,' Lizzie went on with concern. 'He certainly wasn't on my guest list. Chico said he must have been playing polo somewhere in the British Isles and made that his excuse to come to Scotland to cause trouble for you. And the security people let us down. But there'll be no more mistakes, and Pintos won't do anything like that again.' Lizzie's face softened as she stared at Danny and shook her head. 'I feel so guilty about this.'

'Don't,' Danny said firmly. 'Pintos is evil, and I'm glad we're all rid of him.'

Lizzie smiled with relief. 'Thank you for coming back

to the party. That took a lot of courage, Danny. I was so worried about you.'

'You don't need to worry about me. I can look after myself.'

'But we've always looked after each other in the past, haven't we? And I wasn't there for you this time.'

'Lizzie,' Danny said in a mock-stern voice. 'This is your wedding day.'

'And you don't have to put on a front for me, Danny Cameron.'

'I'm not putting on a front. I'm letting this go. I won't allow Carlos Pintos to colour my life, or my thinking, or anything I do.'

'And he won't.' Lizzie gave her a hug. 'But I think there's another man who would like to...'

'Only because you're staring at Tiago. He thinks we're talking about him,' Danny pointed out, tensing as Tiago started heading their way.

She shivered as his shadow fell over them, and then was instantly annoyed with herself for reacting at all.

Tiago made a gracious bow to the bride, and then said, 'Excuse us, Lizzie. Shall we dance?'

Danny almost looked over her shoulder, to see who he was talking to. 'Me?'

'Of course you,' he said.

How could she refuse when Tiago was giving her a look she couldn't misinterpret—a look she had to act on immediately? Chico was hovering, and she had taken up quite enough of the bride's time.

Why make a fuss? she concluded. This was a party. It was no big deal if she had one dance with Tiago Santos.

'Seems I have to thank you again,' she said.

'Why?' He was frowning.

She couldn't speak for a moment as Tiago drew her

into his arms, swamping her with many emotions, chief amongst which was an intense awareness of him. This was more than she had expected to experience in one night. *He* was so much more. It was hard to breathe, or to register anything beyond Tiago's masculinity, and it took all she'd got to concentrate long enough to answer him.

'I'm glad you teased me away from Lizzie. I guess old habits die hard. We've practically been welded to each other since we were children.'

'And then Chico came along?' he guessed.

'That's right,' she admitted, smiling wryly.

'So you and Lizzie have been friends for a long time?'

'Yes, but I should have taken the hint faster that Chico wanted to be with his bride—so thanks for that.'

'Is that why you were in the stables earlier, Danny? Were you wondering how your life would go forward from now on, without Lizzie to confide in?'

'You're too smart,' she said. His intuition was unsettling.

'It's understandable,' he argued, drawing her into his hard-muscled frame so they could dance as one. 'You're bound to consider how this will change things between you, and we all need quiet times to sort out our heads. Did you come to a conclusion?'

She was coming to a few conclusions now. She wished she wasn't wearing such a provocative dress—it was giving Tiago all the wrong signals. He was making her wonder if she had come downstairs too soon.

Her body was rioting at the touch of Tiago's hands and the warmth of his breath on her skin. Having her hand in his was electrifying. Having him direct her movements, even in this harmless dance, was equally disturbing. She had to remind herself that dance was the lifeblood of Brazil, and that it was a means of expression that very few nations could use to such good effect. Right now Tiago and dance had combined to stunning effect.

And she had to keep it up for a little while longer, Danny reasoned, if only because Lizzie was watching them with concern. One dance with the most dangerous man in the room. She could handle that. She wasn't going to allow herself to be intimidated ever again—not by life, and not by Tiago.

They fitted together perfectly, considering Tiago was twice her size. He moved so well he made it easy for her. She found herself moving rhythmically with him in a way that was sexy, even suggestive, but it was just one dance, she reassured herself.

They were close enough to the top table for Lizzie to flash anxious glances their way, and she smiled back to confirm that everything was all right.

And it might have been had she not been moving closer and closer to Tiago. He didn't force her to. His touch remained frustratingly light. But the music was compelling her to do this. It was intoxicating, and the pulse of South America was soon running through her veins. She could feel his muscles flexing as he teased all her senses at once. If she moved away he brought her back.

There weren't many men who looked good dancing, but Tiago was one of them. Maybe because he was an athlete. His body was supple and strong. And he was Brazilian—dark and mysterious and sexy, with a passion he carried everywhere with him. She trembled as he dipped his head and his warm, minty breath brushed her face.

'I didn't know you were such a good dancer, Danny.'

'Neither did I,' she admitted.

His firm lips slanted in a sexy smile. 'It must be because you're dancing with me.'

She laughed at his engaging self-assurance.

'You were such a tomboy in Brazil.'

'I'm still a tomboy, Senhor Santos.'

'Tiago, please,' he murmured, in a husky whisper that raised every tiny hair on the back of her neck.

She couldn't deny she was disappointed to learn that Tiago still thought of her as a tomboy. She was a woman—a woman with needs. She was a confused woman, still recovering from the shock of an attack, but sufficiently recovered to know how deeply this man affected her. And dance was the perfect outlet for her emotions. Dance was a means of expression when words wouldn't come.

When the music faded and the band took a break she felt awkward suddenly, and glanced longingly towards the exit, where the double doors were open wide.

'Have you had enough?' Tiago asked.

She flashed a glance up at him. 'I'm sorry—am I being so obvious?'

'Too much too soon for you, I think,' he said wisely.

Once again that intuition of his was a warning of how easily he could read her. *Tiago* was too much too soon, and always would be, Danny suspected. If she had known how it would feel to be in his arms, how *she* would feel, she would never have agreed to dance with him.

'I do have one suggestion,' he murmured.

'Yes?' She glanced up and felt her heart turn over.

'Just wait a moment before you go. The DJ has taken over from the band, so have one more dance with me.'

She was just basking in the idea that Tiago enjoyed dancing with her when he spoke again.

'That way it will give Chico enough time to make Lizzie forget everything—including you.'

Danny's eyes flashed wide. His comment had stung. That was what happened when she dropped her guard around Tiago Santos. But he was right. She had to let her friend go and move on.

'If you're sure you don't mind dancing with me?' There were so many much prettier girls in the room.

'I'm sure,' Tiago confirmed with an amused look.

This was the type of thing she would have liked to discuss with Lizzie. They had both led such hectic, fractured lives as children, and had protected each other until their lives had been sewn together again by Lizzie's grandmother and by the housekeeper, Annie, both of whom had been determined that neither child would suffer because of their less than responsible parents.

'Shall I get you out of here?' Tiago suggested, after a short time longer on the dance floor.

She refocused fast. 'Sorry—was I frowning?'

'Yes,' he confirmed with amusement. 'I'm disappointed you can't concentrate on me.'

'Maybe that's why I'm frowning,' she suggested with a wry smile.

'Now I'm hurt.'

She doubted that. And she was willing to bet Tiago knew everything she was thinking. But she was starting to feel the strain of keeping up a bright and breezy front after what had happened in the stable.

'Are you serious about getting me out of here?'

'Absolutely,' Tiago said, steering her towards the door.

The other couples on the dance floor quickly closed over the gap they'd left and it was as if they'd never been there, Danny thought as she glanced over her shoulder.

'Don't look round,' Tiago advised. 'Keep on walking. No one will notice we're leaving—I'm thinking of Lizzie now—unless you draw attention to yourself.'

They wove their way through the tables with Tiago's hand resting lightly in the small of her back. His touch was like a lightning transmitter and the force field didn't let up—not even when he drew to a halt in the shadows beneath the staircase in the hall.

'I'll see you to your room,' he said.

She shook her head decisively. 'There's no need for that.'

'But I insist.'

The only explanation she could give for not putting up a better fight was that she was still in a state of shock. Why else hadn't she resisted his suggestion?

When they reached her bedroom door and Tiago opened it for her, he stood back.

'Goodnight, Danny.'

She held her breath as he ran one fingertip lightly down her cheek.

Why had he done that?

'Try to get some sleep,' he suggested gently before she could process that thought. 'This has been quite a night for you.'

In every way, she thought, still tingling from his touch as Tiago turned away.

'Goodnight, Tiago. And thank you...'

She watched him go, and only when his footsteps had faded and disappeared did she realise she was still holding her breath.

CHAPTER THREE

HE NEEDED A WIFE. Danny needed money. He had a plan.
Danny was an intelligent, gutsy woman, and time was
running out for the ranch. He would make her an offer.
Every marriage was a bargain of some sort. People said
they got married for love, but did they never sit back to
think about the benefits to both parties? Not even when
the occasional doubt crept in? Love might make the world
go round, but without money the world and everyone in
it would go to hell in a bucket.

He could offer Danny a shortcut to her dream, while
marriage to her would secure the ranch for *him*. Getting
the amount of money Danny needed for her venture must
seem like a pipe dream to her—but for him…? Money
was the least of his problems.

He'd ask her tomorrow. He'd lay everything out so
she knew exactly where she stood. Their deal would be
secured by a legal contract. And, as a bonus, he wanted
her. He'd wanted her since Brazil.

He only had to think about the families who depended
on him back in Brazil to know this was the right thing to
do. When Danny met them she would agree too.

'Chico?' He had just spotted his friend in a rare moment
away from his bride. It was time to put his plan into action.

'Yes, my friend…'

Chico Fernandez was another powerful polo player, with the dark flashing looks of South America.

Chico placed his arm around Tiago's shoulders. 'What can I do for you?'

'Danny works for you, doesn't she?'

'Danny?' Chico raised a brow. 'You're interested in Danny? She's a pretty little thing. I don't blame you. I'm glad you were able to help her today and, yes, she works here. Why do you ask?'

'I'd like to take Danny back to Brazil with me—if that's okay with you?' he asked dryly.

'Do I have any option?'

'No,' he said flatly, ignoring Chico's black look.

'So you want Danny to come work for you.' Chico's eyes narrowed. 'She's a great rider, and a promising trainer, but you don't need any more staff. What's going on, Tiago?'

'Danny wants her own place, and I think I can help her with that plan.'

'Really?' Chico stared at him suspiciously. 'Danny's had her problems—as you know. Are you going to add to them?'

'That is not my intention.'

'Don't hurt her, Tiago. Please remember that Danny Cameron is my wife's best friend.'

'I want to give her a hand up—that's all. I feel bad for her after what happened today.'

Chico frowned. 'I'll have a word with Lizzie—smooth the way for you.'

'That's all I ask, my friend.'

Danny collapsed with relief on the bed. It was one thing holding it together in public, but now she was here on her own…

Putting her arms over her head, she tried to pretend she didn't want to feel Tiago's arms around her—and a lot more besides. Could she really go through all that heartbreak again, with another polo player? Hadn't she learned her lesson?

Not that Tiago was anything like Carlos Pintos, but he was well out of her league. And how was she supposed to forget how it had felt to be in Tiago's arms on the dance floor? Or how she'd thrilled with pleasure when they'd moved together so effortlessly? How was she supposed to forget that?

She had to forget. She had to file it away with all the other good memories to pull out and reflect on whenever she needed a boost. Tiago was going back to Brazil soon. He would probably be gone by the time she got up in the morning.

While she'd stay here and nothing would change. She would still be working at Rottingdean when she was an old woman—still sending what money she could to her mother. It was never enough. Her mother had no idea about saving, or making do, or even working for a living. But if Danny stayed here she would never have the chance to build a nest egg. She would never own her own place—

So it was time to get moving—get on with life and make as much of a success of it as she could. She had more sense than to waste her time daydreaming about Tiago Santos.

She woke to a chilly grey dawn. Grimacing, she pulled the covers up to her chin. Chico and Lizzie had started improvements on the house Lizzie had inherited from her grandmother, but nothing had been spent on Rottingdean for years, and replacing the entire central heating system in the big old house was still a work in progress. The ancient radiators clanked noisily but gave off little heat—though Danny suspected she was shivering because she was tired as well as cold, having only dozed on and off through the night.

The reason for that was Tiago Santos.

So much for banishing the man from her thoughts! Tiago's touch on her body was as vivid now as it had been when he'd held her on the dance floor. She'd been warm in his arms.

She was a hopeless case, Danny concluded, swinging out of bed. Her only excuse was that Tiago Santos was the type of distraction that could make an arrow swerve from its course.

She showered, and grabbed a towel to rub herself down until her skin glowed red. Clearing a space on the steamed-up mirror, she examined her face. The bruise under her eye had turned an ugly yellow-green. Attractive! But at least the swelling had gone down, thanks to Tiago's horse liniment.

She laughed, remembering the look on his face when she had mentioned the stink. She knew that ointment well. They all used it. It had been a kind thought, but the sort of thing any man would do, she concluded wryly, throwing on as many layers of clothing as she had brought with her. She would have to put on everything she possessed to keep the bitter cold at bay.

It would be warm in Brazil.

'Oh, for goodness' sake!' she exclaimed out loud.

Glancing out of the window, she jumped back fast, seeing Tiago in the yard. So he hadn't gone back to Brazil yet...

With her heart beating like a drum, she took a second look. Tiago had stopped on his way across the yard to speak to a fellow guest, and was being his usual charming self. He made time for everyone, and even from this distance his smile made *her* smile.

It was such an attractive flash of strong white teeth in that stern, swarthy face. It was a smile that made her stomach clench and her limbs melt as she wondered, for the umpteenth time, what it would feel like to have a man like Tiago Santos do more than just hold her in his arms. She had experienced his concern and his friendship, and now she wanted more—she couldn't help herself.

Safe in the knowledge that he couldn't see her looking, she surveyed the well-packed jeans, the calf-gripping riding boots and the heavy sweater he was wearing today—which she found sexy, for some reason—under a jacket that moulded his powerful shoulders to perfection. The collar was turned up against the wind, and with his thick, wavy black hair blowing about he was an arresting sight.

And she should be arrested for what she was thinking.

She stood back quickly when he stared up, as if he could sense her looking at him.

Leaning back against the wall—out of sight, she hoped—she swallowed convulsively and closed her eyes, wondering if she had been too late and he had seen her.

What if he had? There was no law against looking out of the window.

She stole another look. Tiago had quite a crowd around him by this time. Even Lizzie's sophisticated wedding guests were thrilled to chat to a polo player of Tiago's standing, and particularly one whose success on the field of play was almost as legendary as his success with women.

To be fair to him, though, Tiago was also famous for turning his grandfather's failing ranch into a world-class concern. And his relationship with women was none of her business. Which, unfortunately, wasn't enough to stop her thinking about Tiago's women—all wearing outfits composed of cobweb-fine lace, or nothing at all, and smelling of anything other than horse liniment…

She should be going down to breakfast—not staring at one of the wedding guests, Danny reminded herself firmly. She was a home bird—not an adventuress on the hunt for a barbarian mate. She should be outside by now, exercising Lizzie's horse as she had promised Lizzie she would. There was nothing like a ride across the heather to blow the cobwebs from her mind.

Where was Danny? He was waiting to speak to her about his plan. Why hadn't she come down to breakfast?

He glanced at his watch impatiently. Had she made other arrangements? Had he missed her? Had she slipped away without him noticing?

Pushing his chair back, Tiago began to pace the room. Was he wasting his time in Scotland? His manager at the ranch had reported a group of trustees sniffing around Fazenda Santos. In its current condition the ranch was worth a fortune, but if men who didn't know what they were doing took it over it was doomed to fail. He wouldn't risk it—couldn't risk it.

Danny was his best hope if he was to comply with the terms of his grandfather's will, and she had mentioned her frustration at still being here at Rottingdean, where she had worked all her life. Surely she would accept his offer of a scholarship to train in Brazil? But what about the other part of his deal?

'Good morning, Tiago.'

He swung round with relief. 'So, there you are,' he said as she walked into the room

She seemed surprised. 'Were you waiting for me?'

'Yes, I was.'

'Well, here I am,' she said brightly.

A freshly showered Danny, with tendrils of honey-soft hair still damp around her temples, was an arousing sight that forced him to remember that what he needed was a short-term wife. His freedom meant too much to him to consider anything else.

'You seem recovered.'

'I am,' she said, frowning. 'Why wouldn't I be?'

'Good.' That suited him perfectly. 'I trust you slept well?'

Wrong question. His groin tightened immediately at the thought of Danny naked, stretched out in bed. It was important to keep this confined to business. He didn't have much time. But it wasn't easy when she leaned over him to scan the delicious-looking breakfast the house-keeper had laid out.

'I just came to say goodbye to you,' she said, grabbing a piece of toast. 'Annie said you had to get back today. I thought you might have left for Brazil last night.'

She was fishing. He took that as a good sign. 'Sit down?' he suggested. 'Eat breakfast with me. Why are you in such a hurry to get away?'

'Because I'm going riding in a minute. I don't have time to sit down and eat.'

'You'll need something to keep the cold out.'

Her glance flashed over his warm sweater. 'Don't worry about me. I'm wearing Arctic layers,' she explained.

She wasn't joking. She wore a thick-knit sweater with a fancy pattern, heavy winter breeches, and soft tan leather riding boots, which clung tenaciously to her shapely legs, hiding almost all the outline he had delighted in when he had danced with her last night. The thought of unpeeling her 'Arctic layers', as she'd called them, occupied all his thoughts for a moment.

'Why don't we ride out together?'

She stilled, with the toast hovering close to her parted lips. 'Do you have time?'

'I'll make time.'

'In that case...'

He caught her frowning as she headed for the door, as if she suspected there was more to this than a morning ride, but he didn't care what she thought now he had what he wanted.

His spirits lifted. He felt like a hunter with his prey in sight. And why feel guilty when he was about to make Danny an offer she'd be crazy to refuse? There was just one problem. Trying to appeal to Danny Cameron's calculating business brain might be difficult if she didn't have one.

She was quite likely to dismiss his plan out of hand. She would almost certainly consider a marriage of convenience to be selling out, as well as a serious betrayal of the marriage vows—and she'd have no hesitation in telling him. Unfortunately he didn't have the luxury of time to indulge in finer feelings. The thought of trying to do this deal with one of the women he customarily dated frankly appalled him. Even a night in their company could be too long. And where would he find another potential wife at such short notice?

'Riding out will give us chance to chat about your future plans,' he said casually as he held the door for her.

'Advice always welcome,' she said blandly, smiling up. 'But ride first, chat later,' she insisted.

Nothing about this was going to be straightforward, he deduced.

She hadn't planned on riding with Tiago. When Annie had told her he was eating breakfast she had considered going straight out, and then decided that would look cowardly. In keeping with her decision to toughen up, she had decided to face the hard man of the pampas to show him she was over yesterday, and not susceptible in any way to his undeniable charm.

'You're riding Lizzie's horse this morning?' he commented when they reached the stable yard.

'That's right,' she confirmed as they crossed the yard.

The horses were in adjoining stalls. She couldn't pretend that riding out with Tiago Santos wasn't a thrill. And it would look amazing on her CV, she conceded wryly. As if she needed an excuse to ride out with him!

They tacked up together. She tried not to notice how deftly Tiago's lean fingers worked, or how soothing and gentle he was with his horse.

'Are you ready?' he said, turning around.

Her heart-rate soared, and all she could think about was being held in those arms, how it had felt to be pressed up close against his body.

'Ready,' she confirmed, lifting her chin.

She had barely led Lizzie's horse out of the stable when her phone rang. She looked down at the screen and shook her head. 'Sorry, but I've got to take this.'

'Go right ahead.'

She walked quickly away from Tiago, concerned that her mother's torrent of words would alert him to her problem. It was always the same problem. Her mother was short of money again. It was the only time she ever called.

Taking a deep breath, she launched in. 'Did you get my messages? I was worried about you. It seems so long since I've heard from you. Are you sure you're okay? You're *not* okay?' Danny frowned with concern. 'Why? What's happened?'

She dreaded what her mother would say. It was never

good news. The type of men Danny's mother liked to go out with generally needed a loan. She held the phone tight to her ear as her mother repeated the familiar plea.

'It's just to tide him over, Danny. I told him you'd understand...'

Told whom? Oh, never mind. She wouldn't know the man, anyway.

'I knew I could rely on you. Thank you...thank you,' her mother was exclaiming.

'But I don't have that kind of money,' Danny said, horrified when her mother mentioned a figure.

Her mother ignored this comment entirely. 'Just do what you can,' she said. 'You're so generous, Danny. I knew we could rely on you.'

I'm such a mug, don't you mean? Danny thought.

'It's only a short-term loan. He's got money coming in soon.'

How often had she heard that? Danny wondered. 'I'll send you what I can,' she promised.

'I hear there's going to be a lot of money sloshing around Rottingdean now Chico Fernandez has taken control?'

She recognised her mother's wheedling voice and immediately sprang to her friend's defence. 'Chico hasn't taken control,' she argued, feeling affronted on Lizzie's behalf. 'Lizzie and Chico work in partnership, and their money has got nothing whatsoever to do with me. I'll send you what money I can when I've earned it.'

'Make sure you get your hands on some of their money,' her mother insisted, as if she hadn't spoken, and as if Danny were entitled to a share. 'You've got it good now, Danny. It's only fair to share your good fortune with others—with me—when things can only get better for you.'

Her mother's voice had grown petulant and childlike. An all too familiar feeling swept over Danny as she was tugged this way and that by a sense of duty to her mother and a longing to get on with her own life.

'Just one more thing before I go,' her mother said. 'I heard in the village that the repair work at Rottingdean is going to mean evacuating the house soon?'

'That's right,' Danny confirmed. 'It's great news that the old house is going to be given new life, isn't it?'

'I suppose so,' her mother agreed. 'But—and it's really hard for me to say this, Danny—I'm afraid you can't come back here to the cottage while the renovation work is being carried out.'

'Oh?'

'My new fella wouldn't like it, you see. You *do* understand, don't you?'

'Of course,' she said faintly, taking this in.

'I really think he's the one, Danny.'

Another one who was 'the one', Danny mused wearily. 'Just take care of yourself, Mum,' she said softly. She would pick up the pieces of her mother's life when it all fell apart again, somehow. And as for her own—

'You won't forget to send that money, will you?' her mother pressed.

'I promise,' Danny said.

'You're such a good girl.'

Danny shook her head at the irony of her penniless self, bailing out some unknown man, and then the sound of horses' hooves clattering across the cobblestones distracted her. 'Mum—I've got to go. I promised to exercise Lizzie's horse.'

'Just don't forget to send that money, will you, Danny?'

'I won't,' she said again as Tiago rode round the corner, leading her horse.

She cut the line and focused on him. He took her breath away. He looked so good on a horse. He was so at home, so at ease in the saddle, that just watching him was a treat. But she felt anything but at ease, and was already beginning to doubt her sanity at agreeing to ride out with him.

'Important call?' he asked.

'My mother.'

'Nothing more important than that.'

She murmured in agreement, thinking that Tiago looked like a visitor from another, more vigorous planet, with his deep tan, thick black stubble and his wild jet-black hair secured by a bandana for riding. And that gold earring was glittering in the grudging light of the early-morning sun. More marauding pirate, than wealthy and respectable rampaging barbarian…

'Something has amused you?' he asked as he handed over the reins of her horse.

'Just happy at the thought of riding out.' She concentrated on mounting up and curbed her smile.

Just riding out with Tiago would be an adventure—but he didn't need to know that. He made her feel things she had never felt before. Maybe she was a little bit in love with him? *Ha!* Much good *that* would do her.

He gave her an assessing look, but made no further comment as he led the way out of the courtyard.

He was feeling confident as they rode out together. He always felt confident, but Chico had filled him in on Danny's family background, which had led Tiago to believe that if Danny thought she could keep her mother secure *and* have a real chance of starting her own training centre one day her answer to his proposition would be yes.

Urging his horse forward, he headed for the open countryside.

He raised the issue a short time later, when they'd reined in. 'Would you be prepared to leave the country for a good job? Would you be able to leave your mother, for instance?'

'Oh, yes,' she said at once. 'I think she'd be relieved if I left her alone for a while.'

And just sent her money, he thought, remembering what Chico had told him about Danny's mother's constant demands for cash.

'And you? What would you like to do—ideally?'

'Me? I'm still considering my options.'

He ground his jaw as Danny turned her horse, shifted her weight, and took off again. What options was she talking about? Had someone else offered her a job?

He would not pursue her like some desperate adolescent.

Reining in again, he watched her ride. She rode like a gaucho with one hand on the reins, leaning back in the saddle, working her hips, looking as relaxed as if she were sitting in an armchair. She'd learned that in Brazil. She was fearless, he thought as she sped across the brow of a hill. He liked that. He liked Danny. A lot.

He couldn't believe how fate was smiling on him. If he played this right he could have a very enjoyable year with Danny Cameron. Once that year was over she would be free to do as she liked, with all the money she could possibly need, and in the meantime he would enjoy her in his bed.

The only fly in this almost perfect ointment was Danny Cameron herself. He couldn't imagine Danny following meekly where he led. Getting her to agree to a contract of marriage might be tricky, and would certainly require the utmost diplomacy on his part. She might not agree to marry him for cash, but she *would* agree to marry him. He would find a way.

Collecting his reins, he rode after her. The prospect of catching her heated his blood. He needed a result fast. He needed a wife fast. And here she was, perfect in every way: great with horses, and useful on a ranch. What more could he ask of a woman?

CHAPTER FOUR

'YOU'RE QUITE A RIDER,' Tiago commented as they jogged to a halt.

'You mean you couldn't catch me?' she fired back dryly.

'I caught you.'

Her body thrilled at Tiago's warrior glance. She was on a high. If there was anything better than riding out with Tiago Santos she was eager to try it. The fact that she'd given him a run for his money was an added bonus— though she could do without her body purring with approval every time he looked at her. She had to keep her head cool and her thoughts confined solely to horses.

'Have you ever thought of going back to Brazil, Danny?'

Well, that good intention had lasted all of one second. Why did he have to remind her about Brazil, when seeing him had been the highlight of each day? Her thoughts had instantly slipped to the dark side and that fantasy world she inhabited, where she spent nights with Tiago too.

'Maybe,' she admitted. 'It's hard to forget my time in Brazil. All those top-class horses and state-of-the-art training facilities—I can't say I'd turn down an opportunity to go back. Why? Are you offering me a job?'

Tiago remained silent, his considering stare on her face. Maybe she'd overdone it. She was supposed to be exercising Lizzie's horse, not touting for work.

'Shall we get back?' she suggested, wondering if he'd had enough of her company.

'I'm in no hurry.'

And then she understood. He was staring out at the silver river rushing to the sea, beyond which lay a dense and mysterious forest that seemed to beckon them into its hidden interior. There were standing stones that held secrets from ancient times to one side of them, while purple heather spread out like a carpet, leading them home. It was so magical. Who in their right mind would leave?

For a while they sat on their horses in companionable silence. She had loved this vantage spot since she was a little girl. She was at her most relaxed here—until she became aware of Tiago staring at her. What was he thinking? she wondered.

Closing her eyes, she turned her face to the sky and inhaled deeply. Just here, just now, in this one perfect moment, she felt strong and sure—as if things were changing for the better and anything was possible.

'Are you ready to go back now?' Tiago asked.

She was ready for anything. But then she remembered he was heading home to Brazil. That was life. Up one moment; down the next.

'Last one back to the house makes the coffee?' she suggested.

The last sound she heard as she galloped away from him was Tiago's laughter, carried on the wind.

'You're shivering.' he commented when they dismounted in the yard.

'You must be made of iron,' she countered. 'Aren't you

aware that it's a million degrees below freezing today?'
She blew on her hands to make her point.

'Here—let me warm you.'

Before she had a chance to object Tiago had opened
his arms and drawn her inside his jacket. She tensed, and
then reminded herself that Latin men were demonstrative,
that she shouldn't make anything of it. All he was doing
was preventing a mild case of hypothermia setting in.

'Mmm…much better.' Her cheeks were burning as
she pulled away—which she had to do before she grew
used to the addictive feeling of hard, hot man.

'Go inside and warm up in front of the fire,' Tiago
suggested. 'I'll take care of the horses.'

'I'm not leaving it all to you,' she protested. 'We'll do
it together. It will take half the time, and then we can both
take a shower,' she insisted when Tiago seemed about to
refuse. 'You're wet through too,' she reasoned.

Sleeting rain had started to fall at the end of their
ride, in an unrelenting curtain. It showed no sign of easing any time soon.

When the horses were settled they ran for the house.
She screamed as a clap of thunder coincided with Tiago
grabbing hold of her hand to help her run faster, and was
laughing and panting by the time they reached the door.
Just for a moment, as they faced each other and Tiago
stilled, she wondered if he was going to kiss her.

'Come on—let's go inside.'

She spun round before he had a chance. It was a most
unlikely event that he was going to kiss her. She didn't
want to be disappointed. There was nothing worse than
turning your face up for a kiss and receiving nothing.

'Take a shower and warm up,' he told her. 'Then come
back downstairs and we'll talk.'

About what? she wondered. A job? Her heart thundered as she waited for Tiago to reply, but he said nothing.

Brazil.

The thought of returning to Brazil was enough to make her heart race with excitement. The thought of returning to Brazil with Tiago was off the scale. The pampas, the horses, the starry nights, the vibrant music, the warm and friendly people—what she'd give for a chance to go back...

Brazil with Tiago?

Okay. Don't even go there. The thought was so exhilarating she wondered if she'd ever think straight again. But she was never going to make a fool of herself over a man again.

When she came downstairs she found Tiago in the library, where he was standing by the window, staring out into the darkness, seeing nothing as it was so black out there. So he was thinking. But about what? She closed the door quietly behind her, but the click made him turn around. Even now, when she was used to the sight of him again, seeing Tiago Santos here—so tall, so dark, so powerful—she felt her senses flood with heat.

'So, what's this chat you want to have with me?' she said briskly, not wanting to appear too eager. And she had to set her expectations at a reasonable level. Not every interview ended with the offer of a job.

'Sit down, Danny. You're right. I *do* have a business proposition for you.'

She frowned. A business proposition? That sounded a bit formal. What could he mean? She had no money. He must know that. She had no land. He must know that too. She didn't own any breeding stock. She rode whichever horse needed exercise. What could she possibly offer Tiago Santos that he didn't have already in abundance?

Something didn't feel right.

Tiago sat on the sofa facing hers and came right to it. 'I've got a problem—you have too. You need a job,' he said, before she could comment. 'And you need a job that pays a lot more than your work here if you're to have any chance at all of saving to start up your own place.'

'Of course I do—but I'm realistic.' Her laugh was short and sounded false. She didn't like being reminded that her career ambition was probably a hopeless fantasy.

'The type of training stable you envisage running is going to cost a lot of money.'

'I would have to begin small,' she said.

'*Very* small,' Tiago agreed dryly. 'But what would you say if I told you that you don't have to wait, that you don't have to start small? What if I told you that you could do pretty much anything you want?'

'I'd think you were mad—or lying.' She laughed it off, but then something occurred to her. 'You're not saying you'd back me, are you?'

When Tiago had mentioned a business proposition she had never imagined he was considering investing in her skills.

'Yes, that's exactly what I'm suggesting,' he admitted. 'I'd help you to draw up a business plan and I would fund your business.'

She was briefly elated—but then common sense kicked in. 'And what would I have to do for this—beyond training horses and hopefully making a profit eventually?'

She knew full well that establishing a reputation in equine circles would take years. There would be no quick or easy profits for the type of venture Tiago was suggesting.

'You would have to put your faith in me.'

Sitting back, he crossed one booted foot over the other

and with half-closed eyes regarded her lazily, with just the hint of a smile on his mouth.

'What do you mean?' For some reason, instead of feeling excited by Tiago's suggestion, she suddenly felt chilled.

'I'd offer you a contract—a fair contract—that would give us both an out in one year's time.'

'So I could be left high and dry without a job if you felt like it?'

'That would never happen.'

'How can I be sure? What *is* this job?'

Tiago hesitated, and then said, 'As the wife of Tiago Santos you would never be left "high and dry", as you put it.'

'Your *wife*?' She couldn't have been more shocked, and her lips felt like pieces of wood as she spoke the words. 'What on earth are you talking about, Tiago?'

'I need a wife,' he said bluntly, with a careless gesture. 'And I need a wife fast. I'm telling you this because I won't pretend otherwise. I'm going to be absolutely honest with you, so that you know exactly where you stand. The terms of my grandfather's will have left me with no option. I must marry—and soon. Before the trustees find some excuse to take over the ranch. They know nothing of its history—nothing of its people—'

Tiago's passion scorched her. He didn't just care about this ranch and its people—they were his life. That was the only reason she stayed to listen and didn't get up and stamp out of the room. But she was still running his words over in her head. *His wife? Tiago's wife?* She couldn't take it in.

'I'll give you a moment,' he said. 'I can see this has come as a shock to you.'

Tiago was half out of his seat, but she gestured for him to sit down again. 'Please...'

'Don't look so apprehensive, Danny, so alarmed. I mean what I say. You would have everything you've ever wanted—ever dreamed about—right now, rather than waiting, and you'll be secure for the rest of your life.'

Secure? She would be rich enough to own and run her own training establishment—that was a dream come true, just for a start, to someone who had grown up penniless, believing her dreams to be as distant and unachievable as any fairytale. Tiago was offering her the golden chalice.

Yes, but he was keeping it just out of her reach. He could grant her everything—including security for her increasingly unpredictable mother—but at what cost? she wondered.

'I'd be selling out,' she said flatly.

'I'm sorry you see it that way.' Tiago's tone hardened. 'I think if you take a more critical look around you'll see that every marriage is a bargain of some sort.'

'What about love?' She couldn't help herself. She'd always been a romantic. 'Where does love fit into this?' She was as impassioned on the subject as Tiago had been when he'd talked about his ranch. 'I refuse to believe there aren't *some* marriages, at least, based solely on love without thought of gain by either party.'

She could tell he thought her naïve, but she *did* care about love. To love and to be loved was the most important thing in the world as far as Danny was concerned.

'I think we've made a good start,' Tiago continued calmly, as if there'd been no outburst from her.

'And a couple of days in my company is enough time for you to decide you want to *marry* me?'

'We've known each other a lot longer than that, Danny,' he reminded her.

'Yes, but as sparring partners in Brazil—nothing more.'

It had always been a lot more on her part, but she wasn't going to confess that now. She had wanted Tiago from the first moment she saw him, but he had been an international polo player, while she'd been a lowly student living on a grant for young people with troubled home lives. They hardly had anything in common, she'd thought at the time, though that hadn't stopped her standing up to him when he had sought her out. He had loved teasing her, she knew that, and she had loved answering back. It had excited her to confront a man like Tiago Santos and give back as good as she got.

'We've always got on, Danny. If we give this a chance I can see no reason why it can't work.'

'Is that any basis upon which to found a marriage?'

'Better than some,' he said.

Brushing the attraction she felt for him to one side, she challenged him again. 'And is that what you really want, Tiago?'

'I want the ranch.'

Well, that was clear enough.

'I'm proposing you remain married to me for one year, to make it seem genuine. I'm being completely honest with you, Danny. I *have* to get married if I'm to stop those idiots ruining all the good work that's been done on the ranch. Our marriage must be seen as genuine—hence the term I'm putting on it. And, no, I don't want to be tied down. Is that frank enough for you?'

'It *is* honest,' she admitted. 'You want to give me money to induce me to marry you, but you want to carry on your bachelor ways. Is that a fair summary?'

'It sounds rather calculating when you put it that way.'

'How else would you put it? It is calculating. And my answer is no.'

'No?' Tiago's eyes narrowed in disbelief.

'You're suggesting a cold-blooded contract, and yet I have no say in it because you've thought it all through for me. That's right, isn't it, Tiago? You've anticipated what you think it is I want out of the agreement, but you've judged those demands through your own eyes. It must have been very convenient for you, finding me here at the wedding—a brood mare waiting for her stallion. How long have you been sizing me up? Since you found me outside in the mud? Did I look like a victim to you? Did you think I'd be grateful for the crumbs from your table?'

'I never thought that. I would never take advantage of you in that way. I remembered you from Brazil. You were always strong, always determined—'

'And I'm just as determined now to say no.'

Tiago's jaw worked as he mulled over her flat refusal.

'Can I say anything to change your mind?'

She hesitated. Her feelings for Tiago cut too deep for her not to want to help him. She understood that he cared for the ranch, and she couldn't deny that the chance to get to know him better was appealing. But did she have to marry him?

There was something else nagging at the back of her mind—and it was something that was weighted in his favour. The business opportunity Tiago was offering would allow her to *work*—and that was so far removed from anything her mother might do that it did hold appeal. She tried to measure everything she did in life by asking herself: would her mother do it? And if the answer was yes, Danny would do the opposite.

This was her one chance to fulfil her dream, Danny

reasoned. If she could do that, surely she could guard her heart for a year by burying herself in work?

'Well?' Tiago pressed impatiently.

'*If* we go ahead with this—and I'm only saying if—I have certain conditions,' she explained.

His expression turned grim. He wasn't used to bargaining when he had decided what he wanted to do, she gathered, but he could see that she wasn't going to change her mind.

'Name them,' he grated out.

'For one year I'm the only woman in your life. I mean it, Tiago,' she said quickly, when he started to speak. 'I won't take any more humiliation. I've seen my mother make a fool of herself and I don't need anyone to tell me that I was fast following in her footsteps. I won't go down that road again—not for you, not for anyone. If you want this deal you will have to put my terms in that contract too.'

Tension soared as she waited for his reply. She guessed Tiago hadn't expected her to put any obstacles in his way, but she wasn't prepared to back down.

'All right,' he said eventually. 'But if you're putting conditions on this then so am I. This will be a proper marriage, and you will be in my bed.'

Her throat constricted. She couldn't have answered him if she'd wanted to. The expression in Tiago's eyes had turned cold and hard. This was the deal-breaker, delivered by a man determined to have his way. Tiago was like a coin with two sides, she decided. There was the strong and compassionate man on one side of the coin, and the ruthless playboy on the other. Surrendering her body to a man like that was a heart-stopping thought.

But her body betrayed her now by melting. Her mind burned with confusion. It was like drowning in a sweet honey bath of desire, even while everything about Tiago in this frame of mind was a warning to her not to fall for him unless she wanted to be hurt. But how was she going to remain detached from her feelings when she was lying in his arms?

She would have to, Danny determined, but there were one or two more points she wanted to clear up first. 'If this is to be a marriage in every sense, as you suggest it will be, then we have to consider the potential consequences.'

'For instance?' he pressed without warmth.

'How will we explain this love-match of ours to any children we might have? And I use the term "love-match" in its most cynical form.'

Tiago shrugged. 'I must admit I have never thought of this as a permanent arrangement.'

'Clearly,' she said, shrinking a little inside. Was this the one thing in his life that Tiago Santos hadn't thought through? she wondered.

'Finding a wife is uppermost in my mind,' he said, as if he could read hers. 'Perhaps I am guilty of not considering every possibility. I can only tell you that when I found you yesterday outside the stable block I wasn't thinking about this at all. My one thought was your safety. I hope that reassures you? As for this contract— I can't have been planning it for long, *chica*, since I've only been here for a couple of days!'

Calling her *chica* threw her. It was so intimate—too intimate. Endearments from Tiago were unsettling, as was his cold-blooded approach to marriage. When she kept him at a distance she could handle her feelings for him. Jibing at him verbally in Brazil had been fun, but this was a very different situation.

She wasn't about to roll over and become his convenient wife, Danny concluded. Tiago would have to consider her terms and conditions. They were a deal-breaker for her.

'You've only been here for a couple of days,' she agreed, 'but that's long enough for you to negotiate a business contract, I imagine?'

'True,' Tiago agreed. 'But this is particularly important to me.'

'And to me,' she said. 'It's quite a commitment you're asking me to make.' She felt a cold hand clutch her heart as she said this.

Tiago was quick to reassure her, 'The agreement between us will be drawn up by my lawyers to include your demands. It will be absolutely watertight. I assure you of that.'

'I have no doubt.'

'You'll be protected, Danny. You'll be safe. You'll be secure for the rest of your life.'

'You make it sound like a prison sentence.'

'It will be what we make it,' Tiago told her with calm assurance. 'You can have your own lawyers look over the contract. I'll pay for them.'

'But you don't *know* me.' She shook her head, still racked with doubt. 'We don't know each other.'

'How long does it take to know someone? I saw you nearly every day for a year on Chico's ranch. It will be the same. You struck sparks off me with your banter then—'

'Do you mean I stood up for myself?' she asked wryly.

He relaxed, and his mouth curved in the familiar winning smile. 'That's why I like you, Danny. I'm not looking for a push-over. I'm not interested in taking advantage of you. I want this to be fair. And when we're married—'

'I haven't said yes to your outlandish proposal yet,' she pointed out.

'But you will,' he said confidently. 'I will expect you

to stand up to me. I expect you to tell me when something doesn't make you happy. I expect to enjoy a healthy, outspoken relationship.'

'You can depend on that,' she assured him. 'But a year sharing a bed with a man without love…?'

'I'm sorry you see it that way. I wish I had more time to persuade you that this will work really well for both of us, but I don't have that luxury. I can only promise you that you'll have everything you need and that I will always respect you and treat you well.' He shrugged. 'I can't think of anyone I would rather enter into this agreement with—anyone I can imagine seeing on a daily basis and getting on with half as well as I get on with you.'

'So long as we do get on well,' she said dryly.

'Danny—'

'I know. You have a flight plan filed, no doubt, and you don't have time to waste selling love's young dream to me.'

'Don't be such a cynic. It doesn't suit you. Your choice is simple. Stay here and nothing changes, or come with me on the biggest adventure of your life. Which is it to be, Danny?'

CHAPTER FIVE

DANNY TOOK A firmer grip of her suitcase when Tiago threatened to swoop on it. Half an hour ago, over breakfast, he'd shown her the contract his lawyers had drawn up on the screen of his phone. When she had expressed surprise that he had been able to rouse his team at such short notice just before the holidays, he'd set the tone by telling her that holidays were for wimps and that he didn't take them.

Money bought everything, she thought. And now here they were, in the hall, about to leave the house on their way to Brazil. She'd called her mother, but there had been no reply. She hadn't wanted to disturb Lizzie, so she had sent her an email. And her wedding to Tiago...? That lay some time in the future and still didn't feel real.

Just as Tiago had promised, the terms of the contract were solid enough. She'd been given everything she'd asked for, and to build her confidence before she took this final step Tiago had pressed an open first-class airline ticket home into her hands, and told her she could bail out at any time. Yet even now she felt she'd sold out.

Or, as Tiago had so romantically put it, 'Congratulations, *chica*! You've got the guts to seize the opportunity of a lifetime *and* share my bed.'

Yes, she knew he'd been teasing her, in that old, tormenting way, but this time she hadn't fired back. The reality of intimacy with Tiago was only just dawning on her. Yes, of course she knew that intimacy was part of *any* married couple's life, and Tiago had said that their marriage would be as close to normal as it could be for a year, but she was certain that sharing his bed would be very different from her fantasies.

'I said I'd carry it,' she insisted now, attempting to wrestle back her case.

'Too late,' Tiago told her.

Five minutes into the trip and they were already at odds. What did that say about her decision to do this? Tiago was holding the car door open, waiting for her impatiently. There was no going back now. She was leaving everything familiar behind.

Yes, but to embark on an adventure. If she wasn't up to it she had better decide now.

She hurried down the steps to join him.

The car dropped them off at the side of a sleek executive jet, which Tiago and his team would pilot to Brazil, he'd explained. And just in case she was still uncertain as to her status, 'Santos Inc' was written in bold bloodred down the side of the fuselage. She really was entering another world—and it was a faster moving world than she was used to.

'There's no time to hang around,' Tiago insisted, seizing her arm. 'My take-off slot is non-negotiable.'

He wasn't joking. He indicated left rather than right once they were inside the cabin.

'Into the cockpit?' she queried.

'I thought you might like to sit with me when we take off. If you prefer you can sit in the back?'

'No. This is good.' Normally she was a nervous passenger, but since everything else had changed why not this too? 'Thank you...'

Thankfully, she sounded so cool, so certain—but her emotions were in a riot. 'I've always wanted to sit next to the pilot.'

'You won't be sitting next to me. That's the co-pilot's job. But you will still see everything.'

Probably a lot more than she wanted to, Danny thought ruefully, hoping some of Tiago's confidence would wash off on her.

'If you're having second thoughts...it's too late.' He slanted her that dangerous smile that flooded his eyes with amusement and reached all parts of her too. 'There's a bedroom in the back,' he added, 'if you need it.'

'Hopefully not. And I'm not having second thoughts,' she assured him.

'Not yet,' he said dryly. 'It's a long flight, Danny, so go to bed if you have to.'

'What about you?'

'Don't worry about me,' he murmured, with one last look.

They took off smoothly, with Tiago handling the jet with the same easy skill he employed on his horses. When they reached cruising height and levelled off he handed over control of the plane to his co-pilot and came to ask Danny how she'd liked the new experience.

Having turned at just the wrong moment, he caught her chewing her lip as she tried to work out if this was the best decision of her life, or the biggest screw-up ever. It didn't help when she looked at the man who would shortly be her husband. Her body thrilled at the thought, though she still had major concerns.

Flying a jet was all in a day's work for Tiago—as was running a multi-national business and playing polo at international level—while *she* had a neat line in handing out pony nuts, and not a clue when it came to negotiating contracts, let alone those with a marriage clause involved.

She would just have to be a fast learner, Danny concluded as Tiago smiled down at her.

A couple of hours later she was glad to take him up on his offer to use the bedroom in the back of the plane, and was surprisingly snug between crisp white sheets in a very comfortable bed when the door opened.

'Coffee?'

She shot up, and only belatedly remembered to yank the covers to her chin. Having stripped off her clothes, she was naked, while Tiago had rolled back the sleeves of his crisp white shirt, leaving his powerful forearms bare. Her body clenched with pleasure at the sight. There should be a law against being so attractive.

'Sit up,' he urged, putting the coffee down on the nightstand at her side. 'Drink your coffee before it gets cold. Do you have everything you need?'

She wasn't sure she could answer him honestly, and confined herself to a prim 'Thank you for the coffee.'

His lips slanted in a smile. 'Aren't you going to invite me to sit down?'

'No.' When he looked at her like that? Absolutely not.

He sat down anyway. She held her breath as he made himself comfortable. Kicking off his boots, he arranged the pillows to his liking and lay down.

'Are you quite comfortable there?' she enquired sarcastically.

Tiago turned his head to shoot her an amused glance. 'Very. Why?'

Sitting up in bed, she drew her knees up to her chin.

Sipping the steaming coffee, she allowed her hair to cover her face like a curtain, to hide her burning cheeks.

'Am I keeping you?' he growled.

She have him a look. 'From drinking my coffee?'

'I don't know, *chica*. You seem tense to me. Are you naked under those sheets?'

Tiago reached out to hook some hair behind her ear and she exhaled with shock. But then, just as she relaxed, he touched her naked thigh.

'You *are* naked…' His mouth tugged in a lazy smile. 'Silky smooth skin and silky hair.' He wound a strand of her hair around his finger, and then, taking the coffee mug from her hands, placed it safely on the nightstand out of reach.

'Relax,' he murmured, his mouth curving in a smile. 'This is a long flight. Why not enjoy it?'

Because…

Her throat closed down before she could say anything. Tiago's touch was so exciting. He aroused her. He made her want more. Much more.

He took his time to soothe and stir her, and before long she had eased down in the bed as he continued to stroke and kiss her…her arms, her neck, the top of her chest above the swell of her breasts. It all seemed so safe and innocent. He had that down to a tee.

When she opened her eyes it was to find Tiago turned on his side, watching her. To have him monitor her responses aroused her even more, and a shaking breath shivered out of her as his big hand cupped her breast. His palm was so warm and firm, and a little roughened from his work with horses. He had intuitive hands, intuitive fingers, and when he shifted position to move over her, and his dangerous, swarthy dark face blocked out the light—blocked out everything but Tiago—she was more conscious than ever of his size and his strength. And also his willpower, and his control, and that aroused her too.

She held her breath with excitement when he stopped, wondering what would come next.

Making her comfortable on the pillows, he drew the covers back and stared down at her body, and for once in her life she didn't rush to cover herself. She *wanted* Tiago to look at her. She didn't want any secrets between them. She wanted him to see her body respond to him. Exposed like this.

His touch when he stroked her breasts was on another level. She tried to stay still but found it impossible, and with a whimper of need she reached out for him.

Tiago smiled. His dark eyes burned with hunger but he had more control than she had, and even as she writhed beneath him, trying to urge him on, he only dipped his head to brush her lips with his. That was almost enough, that kiss, but he denied her the weight of his body. His kisses fired her, his fingers teased her, and she was agonisingly responsive to his touch, but nothing she could do would make him do more.

He curved a smile. 'I'm the luckiest man on earth.'

She was aching—really aching. She needed his firm touch *now*.

She gasped with relief as he returned to the assault on her senses, using firm strokes across her belly and down her thighs. And all the time he held her gaze in his.

She cried out when his hand finally found its destination. Easing her legs apart, he teased around her clitoris with a touch that was indescribable, while she lifted her hips in a hunt for more contact, crying out in desperation, not caring what he thought. She needed this—needed him. She needed this *now*.

At first she thought he was only going to tease her

and leave her aching, but as if he could sense the level of her need he relented. Using one gloriously roughened finger-pad, he applied just the right amount of pressure, just the right amount of friction, at just the right speed.

Exclaiming at the intensity of sensation, she lost control. Tiago held her firmly in place, using his hand to increase her pleasure and make it last. Even when the pleasure waves began to fade she was incapable of speech, and could only grab a breath as he murmured with amusement, 'I think you needed that.'

He had no idea. Sex as sport might be second nature to him, but she was a novice and would have to put these feelings in her heart to one side.

She laced her fingers through Tiago's hair. His hair was so thick and strong. She loved the feel of it beneath her hands, just as she loved the rasp of his stubble against her neck.

Pressing kisses against her breasts, he eased her down in the bed and at last gave her what she longed for: the weight of his body pressing into hers.

She lost control again. That was all it took. She had imagined this moment for so long that now it was here she could only ride the sensation, while Tiago held her firmly in his arms, dropping kisses on her mouth.

'Good?' he murmured, knowing very well that it was.

'Stop,' she whispered, 'or I won't be held responsible for my actions.'

'Don't be,' he said, finding this amusing. 'Let *me* be responsible for your actions.'

She responded instantly as he teased her into a state of readiness and fell happily into wild release. Tiago's kisses thrilled her. *He* thrilled her. She hadn't realised how fierce she would be when it came to her need for this man. They were a fierce couple. Their hungry kisses spoke of mutual need. Tiago's tongue claimed her. *He* claimed her. He challenged her in a way she welcomed. He made her fight him. He made her test him. He made her feel alive.

When he surprised her by standing up she actually groaned, her disappointment was so extreme, but he didn't lose eye contact with her for a moment, and smiled as he reached for the buckle on his belt.

Folding her arms beneath her head, she rested back, watching him, enjoying the sight of his deft, pleasure-dealing fingers working to free him of the clothes that stood between them. His torso was hard and tanned, muscular, and magnificent, and her body was ready for him. She had never needed Tiago more.

CHAPTER SIX

PLUCKING THE PAGER on his belt off the bed, Tiago scanned it impatiently. 'I'm needed on the flight deck.'

'You have to go *now*?'

He laughed. 'Yes, *chica*—I have to go now. Patience. Put this on the back burner. Save it for our wedding night.'

Once he was dressed he left her, the door closing quietly behind him. She felt like wailing—and not just with frustration. She was angry she had let things go this far. Tiago was so hard to resist, but she needed something more than a quick coupling in the back of his jet. She might not be heading for a proper marriage, as other people understood the term, but retaining some vestige of pride was important to her.

She had lost all semblance of self-respect after her affair with Carlos Pintos, and she knew what a long walk it was back. This time she wanted to come out of it with her head held up high.

Collapsing on the pillows, she groaned. It would be hard coming back from this. Not only would Tiago expect more from her in the physical sense, but the way she felt inside her heart gave 'aching with need' a whole new meaning. Her body ached too, but even that couldn't compare with the inner pain.

Tiago had awoken dreams and thoughts and feelings inside her—more than she'd known she had.

Tossing and turning, she curled up into a ball and tried to sleep. It was useless. Nothing worked. And it wasn't just thinking about what might have happened with Tiago that was keeping her awake. There was so much she didn't know about him, so much she wanted to know. Maybe in Brazil they'd get the chance to talk—hopefully before their wedding night. She didn't even have a clue when that would be. She really had jumped in with both feet this time.

If Danny had thought Chico's ranch in Brazil was fantastic she was in for a surprise when they arrived at Fazenda Santos, where *everything* was impressive—from the immaculately maintained fencing, stretching as far as the eye could see over rolling green pampas, to the state-of-the-art buildings that comprised the stud. Tiago's ranch was situated in one of the wildest regions on earth, allowing her to gain a far better understanding of the scale of his work.

Tiago seemed not to need anything as mundane as sleep, and after a shower said he would be checking round the ranch. Or at least that part of it closest to the house, he explained, as surveying all of it would take a month or more.

'When I return I will have a hard copy of our contract with me,' he promised, leaving her in the capable hands of his friendly housekeeper, Elena.

She was alone now in her bedroom, with time to reflect on the rapidly unfolding events of the past few days. She made a start on investigating the suite of rooms, knowing she should unpack and bathe, take the chance to go to bed for a few hours, but she just couldn't. She was too tightly wound.

Seeing Tiago's home for the first time was like opening a box of surprises, and she'd soaked up every detail greedily. She wasn't sure what she had expected. Not some grungy living quarters on a ranch devoted to raising ponies, because Tiago's playboy side would never allow it. But not glitz and glamour either, as that wouldn't be appropriate for a working ranch, and for all his society polish Tiago was a surprisingly down-to-earth man.

The reality was a happy mix between comfort and luxury. The ranch house was a large, rambling building, and when they'd first driven up to it Danny wondered if he lived in just a small part of it—perhaps a bachelor pad, stark and functional, with just the high-end accessories of life to keep him company. She had pictured high-tech gadgets jostling with spurs and boots, fast cars parked outside, maybe a Harley. She wouldn't have been surprised to see saddle soap and tins of hoof oil on the kitchen table, or bridles slung over the banister in the hall.

She couldn't have been further off-beam. Tiago's home was a stunning example of an old-style ranch house, though it certainly boasted every conceivable modern facility. In spite of its size he had managed to make his home cosy. Mellow wood predominated, along with all the colours of the earth—russet, ochre, claret and dusky blue—which, with the wooden floors and ethnic wall hangings, gave the old house a prosperous look and an ambience she found as alluring as Tiago.

She should have known he would live comfortably, Danny reflected as she walked to the window to stare out down the long, impressive drive. The gates had been the first giveaway that she was entering somewhere really special. They were impressive, carved out of centuries-old wood, and they had opened on to a scene of well-ordered prosperity. The drive up to the house was broad and long, and impeccably groomed, with paddocks full of horses either side. Immaculate farm buildings stood in the distance, together with a host of other facilities she had yet to name.

But even the buildings hadn't impressed her as much as Tiago's wonderfully welcoming staff. They'd shown her nothing but warmth and enthusiasm since the moment she'd arrived, and she had noticed Tiago's face lighting up like a flame when he had received their smiling welcome to his home.

'These are my people, Danny,' he had told her, with such pride in his voice.

She'd never seen him so animated. And then he'd made the introductions, leading her by the hand as if they were already married. Whatever reservations she'd had about their unusual arrangement had faded then. How was she supposed to keep her heart out of this, surrounded by such warmth?

But she wasn't an employee, and she wasn't Tiago's fiancée either. She was in an odd position, Danny mused as she continued to explore her accommodation. There was a lavish dressing room that had obviously been equipped in anticipation of visitors with a far more sophisticated lifestyle than she had. She wondered again what Tiago's staff must make of her, and then put it out of her mind. It was up to her to form a bond with this place, and with its people, and an arbitrary title wouldn't help her to do that.

What she loved most, Danny decided, turning full circle, was the lack of ostentation. There was just sheer quality everywhere she looked. Inside, the house was perfect, while outside the emerald-green pampas beckoned.

Her bathroom wouldn't have been out of place in the most sumptuous hotel. The cream marble was veined with honey, and there were more fluffy towels than she could count. She paused to stare out of the bathroom window, from where she had a good view of the rolling paddocks and the formal gardens surrounding the house. They had flown over Tiago's ranch for miles, he had explained, before he'd brought the jet in to land.

She had been shipwrecked on a desert island fit for a queen.

Her upbeat mood changed abruptly when she remembered Tiago's parting words. Even here, in this cosy suite of rooms, a shiver ran through her. She had been telling him how much she loved his home when he'd replied, 'This is what money can buy, *chica*. This is what *you* can buy now.'

It all came down to the ranch for Tiago, and he thought she felt the same about money.

When Tiago returned from his tour of the ranch everything moved towards the wedding at breakneck speed.

'I had wanted time for you to get used to your surroundings,' he explained the next morning with a careless gesture, 'but there *is* no time. The clock is ticking. I must marry before the week is out if I am to fulfil the terms of my grandfather's will.'

And there was no chance he would risk reneging on that, Danny thought, though now she'd met the people on the ranch she could understand why.

'Will there be enough time to arrange everything?' she asked with concern.

'You knew the terms of our agreement before you left Scotland,' Tiago said impatiently, ruffling his thick black hair.

'Yes, but—' She pulled herself up. 'I hadn't expected it to be quite so soon.'

'I factored in the inconvenience element when I calculated your payment.'

His words hurt. Tiago could be charm personified, or he could be as he was now—a warrior, ruthless and driven, a man who had paid a lot for his bride. And now it was payback time.

She had to remind herself that this wasn't a love-match but a marriage of convenience—for expediency, and to ensure her mother's future as well as her own.

They were standing in a field where foals were grazing, and she guessed Tiago had brought her here on purpose, so she would be relaxed when he dropped the bombshell of their marriage happening by the end of the week. He must have known how quickly they would have to be married before they'd left Scotland, but had chosen not to tell her. Perhaps because he'd been worried that she'd change her mind.

Her hope for a happy-ever-after future had always been slim, but now it drained away into the ground.

Sensing her tension, Tiago wheeled around to pin her with a stare. 'I thought I had explained quite clearly the urgency of this situation?'

'You did.' She was a 'situation' now.

'We should get the contract signed.'

'Yes.'

She would sign. She wouldn't go back on her word. She would make the best of this *situation*, and commit to a life she couldn't imagine. It would be a life with the man who had won her heart in Brazil, but a life in which she neither belonged, nor would be able to distance herself.

When Tiago started walking back towards the house his face was set. 'Let's get this thing done. I want you to check the contract over carefully—make sure you agree with all the terms before you sign.'

How cold-blooded could a wedding be?

She was about to find out.

She had always had such soft, romantic dreams about her wedding day...the wildflowers she would wear in her hair. Everyone would walk to the kirk in the village of Rottingdean and there would be a party afterwards in the village hall. Everyone would help out and contribute something. It would be such a happy day—a simple day, a precious day full of memories...the type of memories she would treasure for a lifetime.

That was her dream. The facts were somewhat different. It sounded as if there was going to be a rushed ceremony—possibly with witnesses she didn't even know.

Tiago was striding ahead of her. His transformation into gaucho was complete. The unforgiving pampas had carved him. Even his clothes had changed. There was nothing designer about his clothes now—nothing of the playboy. He wore threadbare jeans with worn leather chaps over them, and a red bandana secured his wilful hair. His boots were tooled leather, and he carried a lethal-looking *facón*—the vicious knife that gauchos wore—hanging from their belt.

It was hardly possible to believe that this rock-like individual was the same sophisticate who had joked and laughed and made her feel good about herself on Chico's ranch.

Tiago had stopped abruptly—but not to wait for her. He was staring at some horses in the field—evaluating them, counting them, maybe, though she suspected he knew every head of stock. Compared to his ranch, she was nothing. There were no sacrifices Tiago would not make, no lengths he would not go to, to keep this land.

She could always change her *mind.*

Could she? Signing this contract was a way forward for her—the best and perhaps the only way to secure her mother's future.

'Now you understand why I must do this,' Tiago said with confidence as he laid the contract down in front of Danny on his desk. 'You've only seen a fragment of the ranch, but enough to know that it must be saved.'

She wouldn't disagree with him, Danny thought as she took her time to check the contract, line by line. It was everything she had asked for, everything she had read on the screen of his phone—not a line had been changed.

'A year...' she murmured, wondering if it would be a happy year, or a year of torment for them both. And then something mischievous occurred to her, right out of the blue. 'How many relationships have you had that have lasted a year, Tiago?'

He narrowed his eyes and she could practically see his hackles rise. 'I don't understand what that's got to do with this.'

'How many?' she pressed.

Raking his hair with an impatient gesture, he decided to ignore her question. 'Are you going to sign this or not?'

She guessed he had *never* stayed with a woman for as long as a year. Tiago was sailing into uncharted waters as much as she was. If he had ever enjoyed a long-term relationship the press would have seized on it. What the press would make of their marriage she didn't know—and didn't care, either. This was a private arrangement between the two of them. The world would have to make of it what it wanted.

He held out his pen. She took it and signed her name, and Tiago countersigned the document after her. She stared at their signatures and felt cold inside. She had no idea what Tiago felt. Relief, certainly, but she doubted whether he felt anything more.

What had made him this way? she wondered. The polished playboy of the polo circuit seemed far happier and more relaxed here on his ranch, working alongside the gauchos. The thought that she had just contracted to marry a man she didn't know did nothing to reassure her. She should have listened to those rumours of the lone wolf. If she had she wouldn't be here now, with her heart yearning for a man who thought of her only as the means to an end.

'So you're rich now,' he said. 'How does that feel?'

'Strange,' she admitted.

Stranger still was the fact that she had never felt more impoverished in her life.

What had she done? Danny wondered as she watched Tiago cross the yard. She had to shake off this feeling of doom. She was about to join one of the finest horsemen in the world and work alongside him. What could be better than that? The wedding would happen when it happened, and in the meantime she would concentrate on everything Tiago could teach her about the ranch.

Maybe that would bring them closer. If not love, then maybe they could pick up their friendship and make the year ahead bearable for them both. That shouldn't be too hard when they shared so many interests.

Deciding to act as if this were just a new and exciting day in Brazil, rather than the start of a new and uncertain life, she leaned over the fence of the corral where Tiago was working, telling herself that she would get through this, and would learn a lot along the way.

'Would you like to try?' Tiago called to her softly.

He didn't take his attention off the young colt he was training for a moment. The pony was trembling with awareness, and it was one of the most valuable animals on the ranch, Tiago had explained.

'You'll let me work with him?' Danny asked with surprise.

'Why not? You're good.'

She couldn't pretend that didn't thrill her.

Taking care to shut the gate silently, she joined one of the best horse-trainers in the world. Working alongside Tiago would be the greatest opportunity of her life.

'Now, watch how I do this,' he said after a few moments.

Watching Tiago was no hardship. She watched his lips move when he spoke. She watched the muscles flex in his arms as he worked with the pony. She watched his hands soothe and stroke with exquisite sensitivity—

'Concentrate,' he said softly.

She hated it that he knew what she was thinking.

'That's good, Danny.'

He came to stand behind her. She held her breath as his body brushed hers, and tensed when his hands came around her, allowing Tiago to use his hands to direct hers.

'Bring your face closer,' he advised in an undertone. 'Share the same air as your pony.'

His husky voice was hypnotic, and his touch made both Danny and the pony relax.

'He's starting to trust you,' Tiago murmured. 'I'm going to move away now, while you carry on. Caress him, speak to him and build his confidence. Who knows? One day he might be yours.'

Danny smiled, knowing she would never be able to afford the young colt, and then felt a spear of surprise, knowing that with Tiago's marriage settlement in the bank she could.

'What would you call him?' he asked.

'Firefly.' She turned, expecting to find Tiago behind her, but he was already with the gauchos on the other side of the fence.

He was on the same wavelength as Danny, Tiago reflected as he watched her work. He never allowed bystanders into the corral when he was working with young ponies fresh to training, but he trusted Danny. He'd seen her work on Chico's ranch.

And on the personal front...?

He trusted her on the personal front too. He couldn't say that about any other woman apart from Elena, his housekeeper. His mother had been a socialite—a butterfly who had fallen in love with the son of a rough working man who'd happened to own a valuable ranch. His mother had seen an opportunity.

Tiago had been pampered and petted as a boy—a situation he'd refused to tolerate as a teen. By that time his father had been a drunk and his mother an ageing beauty who had refused to accept that her day in the sun was over. There had to be more pills, more potions, more clothes, more visits to the beauty salon, and then eventually to the plastic surgeon. She had ruined his father, who had ended up stealing from the ranch, leaving Tiago's grandfather with nothing.

It had taken Tiago to return—a changed man—and rescue things to the point where Fazenda Santos had become no longer a broken-down ranch that existed solely to feed the greed of his parents, but a highly successful concern he had dedicated his life to.

Did he *want* to get married, with a family history like that?

No. But a year with a woman as lithe and lovely as Danny might just be tolerable—especially when she was in his bed.

CHAPTER SEVEN

TIAGO WAS IN a good mood after working with the colt, and as they walked back to the house it seemed as good a moment as any for Danny to ask him about the details of the wedding. She might not be having the idyllic country wedding she had imagined as a girl, but arrangements would still have to be made. It might be a hastily arranged formality, or—and she desperately hoped this wouldn't be the case—a full-blown society wedding for the type of people Tiago mixed with when he was on the polo circuit.

'So…our wedding…' she began.

'Friday,' he said.

'Friday?' She looked at him blankly.

'Friday is the end of the week,' he said impatiently. 'I did tell you it would have to be this week.'

Yes, but talking about something was very different from facing the reality of the situation. She was already running through a checklist in her mind.

'There's too much to do in the time available.'

Even if a wedding could be arranged at such short notice, she had to consider the demands of the ranch, as well as the Thunderbolts' polo fixtures.

'Did you check on the team's games?'

'Of course.' Tiago drilled a stare into her eyes, as if

the choice between a polo match and their wedding was no contest. 'All we need for this wedding is you and me and a couple of witnesses.'

'I never expected anything more,' she said, angry to think Tiago imagined she craved some sort of grand ceremony to accompany her pay-out.

Nothing could be further from the truth. It was bad enough knowing she had to make promises that she would only keep for a year, without attempting to fool wedding guests into believing theirs was a romantic love match.

'We'll get married here on the ranch,' Tiago said, to her relief. 'But I want everyone to share the celebrations. This won't be a quiet wedding. I'm not ashamed of what we're doing, and neither should you be. When Chico and Lizzie return from their honeymoon we'll fly to Scotland and have a blessing at the kirk in the village, with a party afterwards. You can have whatever you want, then—ten dresses and a dozen bridesmaids, if you like.'

Tiago knew so little about her, she thought, chilled by his casual attitude. 'I just want to get it over with,' she said, speaking her thoughts out loud. She was uncomfortable discussing the charade they were about to take part in.

'I am not trying to cheat you, but I do want you to understand this situation for what it is. It's a short-term solution that will benefit both of us enormously.'

'I know that. I've made a bargain and I'll stick to it,' she confirmed.

Tiago relaxed. 'Thank you, Danny.' And then his eyes became slumberous, and a half-smile curved his wicked mouth. 'Our wedding must be soon. I don't *do* waiting.'

For anything, she remembered, thinking about their encounter on his jet.

'I suggest you get some rest between now and Friday, *chica*. It will be a big day for you.'

And an even bigger night, she thought, shivering in a very different way.

'Will I see you before then?' She tried to sound casual, and only succeeded in making Tiago impatient.

'I hope you're not trying to tie me down even before we're married?'

'No.' She took him on. 'I'm asking you a question.'

'Will the fire of South America sit well with the frost of Scotland?' he mocked.

She raised a brow. 'Let's be quite clear. I've got no intention of becoming your doormat.'

'Well said,' he approved, curving her another smile. 'And now I have business to attend to. You'll see me when I get back.' His powerful shoulders eased in a careless shrug. 'I can't tell you how long that will be.'

'So long as you're back for our wedding, I imagine that will be time enough,' she said coolly.

Tiago huffed a laugh. 'I wouldn't miss it for the world,' he assured her.

Those eyes, that smile—she was glad he couldn't feel the heat surging through her veins. To say Tiago was arrogant would be vastly understating the case, but he was also bone-meltingly hot, and she was in no way immune to his appeal.

'Shall I spread the word about our wedding?' she suggested mildly.

'Tell anyone you like.'

'Fine. Goodbye, then,' she said coolly. 'Enjoy your trip.'

Tiago stared at her as if he expected something more —a longing look, perhaps, or a flaccid wave. She gave him a steely look as he walked away, and then—not for the first time—wondered what on earth she had got herself into.

It wasn't as if she couldn't arrange a wedding, Danny reasoned, now that she was alone, but for all Tiago's interest in the matter it was clear to her that the groom intended to carry on as usual, with no interruption to his schedule. She could challenge him all she liked, but Tiago wouldn't change his life for anyone.

He would be back by Wednesday, thought Tiago. She could like it or not. He *would* be back—because the gauchos were holding a party on Wednesday night, and he would take the opportunity to introduce Danny formally as his intended bride. And then he would take her to bed.

Everyone would know by then, as she would have told them, and waiting until their wedding night on Friday was too long for him to wait to claim a woman he'd already tasted and been denied.

He'd made a good deal with Danny and he was confident she would stick to it. It pleased him to think the people on the ranch already liked her. And the gauchos wouldn't have crowded around to watch her training the colt if she hadn't been good. The sketchy character he'd drawn in his mind of the wife he would be forced to take had acquired an appealing reality in Danny, and if their brief encounter on the jet had been anything to go by she would be a willing pupil outside the training ring too.

Tiago was a saint. That much she had learned while he'd been away. As she crossed the yard on Wednesday morning, heading for the house, she was still thinking about her conversation with one of the elderly gauchos, who had told her that Tiago rarely took time off. He knew every family by name, and all the names of generations past.

He'd saved them from ruin, having plucked his grand-father's property from the brink of disaster. His parents had both been fools, who hadn't been able to spend Tiago's grandfather's money fast enough. They had been more interested in funding their lavish lifestyle than in saving the ranch.

The old man's face had lit up at this point as he'd told her, 'But Tiago is different. Tiago is one of us.'

Tiago was overly generous to everyone who worked for him, and one of the most highly regarded horse-trainers and horse-breeders of his time. He was also a world-famous polo international.

Basically, he had no flaws—though Danny suspected the world's women might disagree, because Tiago had never recovered from his mother's spendthrift ways and so didn't trust women. This was what Elena, who had a far better command of English than anyone else on the ranch, had explained, after hugging Danny when she'd heard about their impending wedding.

Tiago's mother had been the sophisticated type, Elena had confided, and she had groomed her son to be a play-boy. This was a mask Tiago still wore when it suited him, but he was gaucho through and through—like his grand-father before him.

Danny took all this information and added it to what she already knew about Tiago, but whether it would give her more confidence regarding the next year or less, she wasn't sure. Tiago was a product of his upbringing, and *she* was hardly a child from a stable home. Perhaps together they stood a chance of building something worth-while?

They might, but that wasn't why she was here. In a year's time there would be no Tiago and Danny together. What was the point of building anything beyond an understanding between them?

Hearing rotor blades, she stopped in the middle of the yard to stare up at the sky. *He was back.* Her heart thundered. She tightened her grip on the parcel in her hand. She had bought him a wedding gift—had it made for him by one of the gauchos on the ranch. It was only a small gesture, but it was something. She didn't want to go to Tiago empty-handed on Friday.

Now she began to wonder why she'd done it at all, and what he'd make of the gift—this man who could buy anything, and who travelled to town in his helicopter.

She glanced at the bulky package and at the white knuckles on her hand. Sucking in a deep, steadying breath, she firmed her resolve. Why go for half-measures?

Plucking a flower from one of the pots in the yard, she tucked it beneath the string on the parcel. Whether Tiago wanted her or not, he'd got her for a year—and she'd got him.

And he took her breath away.

Tiago's air of purpose and energy seemed redoubled as he strode into the yard. He didn't waste time. Dragging her close, he stared into her face for a heartbeat, and then kissed her as if he would never let her go.

'I've missed you,' he growled. 'Where's Elena?'

Still recovering from his sensory assault, she somehow found the breath to tell him that the housekeeper had gone home about an hour ago.

'Excellent.'

Maintaining eye contact, Tiago backed her towards the house. Removing the parcel from her hands, he left it on the hall table along the way. He grabbed her hand when they reached the foot of the stairs.

'No!'

He stopped abruptly and stared down at her, frowning. 'No? What do you mean, *no*?'

'I mean no.' She had to tell him how she felt about this. 'I don't want to.'

'You don't want to what?' Tiago demanded, his expression darkening.

'I don't want to make love to you. Not today. Not now.'

He seemed incredulous, and laughed. He certainly wasn't used to rejection. 'Explain,' he said coldly.

Stiffening her resolve, she went ahead and told him. 'I have decided to save myself for our wedding night.'

His frown deepened, and then he laughed again. 'You've *what*?'

'You heard me. I'm not going to bed with you until our wedding night. I want to make it special,' she explained, starting to feel awkward as Tiago stared at her as if she were mad.

'I have to keep my pride, Tiago. Surely you understand that?'

'Your pride?' His eyes narrowed.

'Yes, my pride,' she insisted more forcefully.

Tiago lifted his hands away from her, as if the last thing he wanted now was to touch her.

'Please don't be angry.'

He stepped back. 'Is this some sort of power-play?' He stared down at her suspiciously. 'Are you using sex as a weapon?'

'Hardly. I'm not using sex at all.'

He was incredulous. He didn't have a clue what could be motivating this. Danny had been so different on the jet. But as he advanced towards her she paled, and put her hands flat against his chest.

'Please…' she said, staring up at him.

What had he been thinking? Was he no better than

Pintos? Had his desire for Danny blunted his brain entirely?

The world he inhabited was brutal and unforgiving. The brand of polo he played was more than competitive, it was aggressive. But aggression had no place when he was with Danny. Losing had never been an option for him, whether that be in the game of polo or the game of life. But Danny was different, and she required different rules. He'd been drawn to her in Brazil because she'd been fun to be around, but the more time he spent with her the more he realised just how badly she'd been hurt, and how well she hid that hurt.

And now he was going to add to it?

They stared at each other, and then he said, with a reluctant shrug, 'I guess waiting until our wedding night could be a good idea.'

'Liar,' she whispered, smiling now. But then she added softly, 'Thank you, Tiago. Thank you for understanding.'

'Me?' He smiled into her eyes. 'Understand pride? I'm surprised at you, Danny. You should know I'm an expert on the subject.'

She exhaled raggedly and, having surmounted that hurdle, went on to the next. 'I've got something for you,' she revealed.

'For me?' Tiago couldn't have looked more surprised. 'Why have you bought something for me?'

Was she the first woman ever to buy him a gift?

'Why shouldn't I buy something for you?' She was genuinely bewildered. 'I wanted to thank you.'

'*Thank* me?' Tiago's lips pressed down in puzzlement as he stared at her. 'For what?'

'For the chance to work alongside you—the chance to live here on your ranch for a year.'

Danny's heart filled as she spoke. There were so many

reasons to thank Tiago, starting with right back at the stables in Scotland, when he had saved her from Carlos Pintos. And now he had understood why waiting until they were married before having sex mattered so much to her.

Even further back, in Brazil the first time, when she had still been raw from her disillusionment with Pintos the first time around, it had been Tiago she'd always looked for—and not just because he was the most attractive man on the ranch…though that fact had been hard to ignore. He'd always been able to lift her spirits. He had made her feel relevant again when Pintos had called her a waste of space, and she had believed him. Tiago had never seemed less than pleased to see her, and he had made her feel like someone worth seeking out for a chat.

'Watching you work has been a revelation for me,' she said honestly. 'Having this chance to meet the people you work with, to learn how they live, will be a privilege.' She shook her head as she struggled to find the right words. 'I'd work here for nothing for the chance to learn from you.'

'You haven't mentioned money once,' he said—more as an observation than a criticism.

'Why would I?' Her elation dwindled as she remembered that this had always been about money for her. No wonder he was cynical. They both had a long way to go to build any trust between them.

'So what did you buy me?' he wanted to know.

She was glad of the change of focus, but embarrassed that her gift was small in comparison to the riches Tiago was used to. 'I think you can safely call it a job-appropriate gift.'

'What?' he demanded. 'A tin of hoof oil?'

Danny smiled. 'Not exactly.' Leaving his side, she

went to collect the bulky parcel he'd taken out of her hands. 'I just hope it's okay.'

The gaucho who had made the special coin belt for her had explained that in the olden days these traditional belts decorated with silver coins had been used almost as portable bank accounts for gauchos, as they moved from place to place in search of work.

'Now I'm curious,' Tiago admitted as she pressed the package into his hands.

'So open it.' She stood back, relieved that the tension between them had eased—at least for now.

'*Deus*, Danny, this is really special.' Tiago handled the belt reverently, the silver coins chinking in a smooth riff as they passed through his fingers. 'I can't thank you enough.'

'Do you really like it? It's not too much?'

'I love it. It's perfect,' he insisted. 'And I love you for thinking of it.'

He loved her.

No. Tiago didn't love her, Danny reasoned, losing patience with her romantic self for allowing that thought to slip through. He loved her for thinking of him and for choosing the belt.

'Manuelo said you'd like it.'

'Manuelo helped you with your choice?' He seemed impressed by this. 'Manuelo must like you. He and his family have been making these belts for generations, but he won't make them for just anyone. These traditions are another reason why this ranch is so special to me.'

'You don't have to tell me how much this ranch means to you.'

Catching her close, Tiago kissed her—first on each cheek and then, after a pause, on her mouth. He had never kissed her like that before. It was a tender, lingering kiss that made her eyes sting with tears, and when he pulled back there was a look in his eyes that thrilled her. It was warm and assessing and thoughtful.

'What?' she prompted when he didn't speak.

He slanted her a smile. It planted that attractive crease in his cheek. 'I bought something for *you*,' he revealed. 'I hope you like it. I went shopping in town.'

She smiled back at him as she imagined Tiago battling with the crowds. 'Now, *that* I would like to have seen.'

'I bought you this…' Reaching into the back pocket of his jeans, he brought out the most astonishing diamond ring. 'Do you like it?'

She was too stupefied to speak. And when she did find her voice she could only blurt, 'You kept *that* in your back pocket?'

'The boxes were boring,' Tiago said, frowning. 'They were all the same. What's the point of them? Everyone has them. I'm not everyone—and neither are you. If you don't like it I'll change it.'

She turned the fabulous ring over in her hand, hypnotised by the prisms of light flashing from it.

'What?' he said. 'You don't seem keen. Is it too big? Too small? Too sparkly?'

Relaxing at last, she laughed. 'I'm sorry. I don't seem very grateful, do I? It's absolutely beautiful, Tiago, but I can't accept it.'

'Rubbish,' he flashed. 'But just in case…' He reached into his jeans again. 'I bought a few more, in case you didn't like that one.'

She gasped as he tipped a selection of rings into her hand to join the first. Each was a fabulous jewel in its own right, and there was every possible style, colour of stone and variety of cut.

'Take your time,' he said with a shrug, as if he had

given her a selection of candy to choose from. 'Or keep them all, if you prefer.'

Wealth on this scale was incomprehensible to Danny. 'But I don't understand...'

'What's to understand?' Tiago demanded. 'We're getting married. I want my wife to have the best.'

'Yes, but...' She hesitated, knowing she would rather have a tender word from him, or a teasing look like those they'd used to share in Brazil. This felt like another payment—a bonus to secure the deal.

'This is a gift,' Tiago said, as if reading her mind. 'My gift to you.'

She still wasn't convinced. Had all his mistresses received similar gifts? Suddenly the rings felt cold and heavy in her hand.

'I can't keep them.'

'Of course you can.' Tiago closed her hand around them. 'Keep them all. Swap them round from day to day, and then you'll never be tired of them.'

'I can't do that.' She was genuinely shocked. 'I can't casually swap these rings around as I might change my clothes. Any ring you give me is going to be a precious keepsake and full of meaning. Its value will lie in more than the stone.'

He frowned. 'So you don't like my gift?'

'I didn't say that. I love them. But all these are too much. You don't have to do this, Tiago. Under the circumstances, wouldn't it be more appropriate if you gave me something simple? Or nothing at all. I don't *have* to have a ring.'

'I want you to have a ring,' he insisted.

'Because of what other people might think?' she suggested.

'I don't give a damn what other people think,' he

flared. 'Take the rings. Sell them if you don't want to wear them—put the money towards stock for your new premises, if that's what you want to do.'

His voice had turned cold. She could tell she had hurt him. Her heart shrank at the thought. They were so close, and yet miles apart.

'You're a very generous man, Tiago' she said quietly, closing her hand around the rings. 'Thank you.'

'Good,' he said briskly, as if he were glad to have the matter dealt with.

CHAPTER EIGHT

SHE WAS FALLING in love with this man, Danny realised as they rode out side by side later that day. But how could she ever relax totally with Tiago, the gaucho who made her laugh and who had taught her so many things about horses, when she had to handle his cold-blooded play-boy side too?

That would have to be a problem for another day, she concluded as he looked at her.

He glanced at their horses. 'Shall we test them?'

'Why not?'

His dark force was irresistible. Tiago's love of challenge and risk and danger was fast becoming her secret pleasure. The heat and passion of Brazil must have infected her, she realised as they urged their horses on. The sun was warm, the breeze was cool, and scent from the flowers they were trampling saturated the air she breathed. There surely could be nothing more exhilarating than this. Nothing that could release the tension inside her faster.

Except for one thing, she thought as she flashed a glance at Tiago, who looked so relaxed, and yet so dark and dangerous in the saddle—and that would have to wait until their wedding night.

Tiago reined in beside the river that watered his land,

and for a moment she allowed herself to believe she needed nothing more out of life than this. She could work alongside Tiago for a year without wanting him to feel the same way she did.

Couldn't she?

He had never looked better than here, where there were no pretensions, no dress shirts, no tailored suits— just Tiago in the raw, in ripped and faded jeans, with battered leather chaps over them, a faded top clinging to his hard-muscled torso, and a bandana tied carelessly around his wild black hair.

She was rapt as he pointed things out to her. The giant-sized Rhea bird, disappearing into the long grass, and a wild cat that surprised her by diving into the river as Tiago explained that this particular breed of cat ate frogs.

He turned to her. 'This is a nature reserve. All the animals are safe here. My vets are responsible for them just as they are for my horses.'

She was learning a lot—and not just about the animals. Hearing about Tiago's interests and his active concern for this land told her more about him than anyone could.

'Last one to the house makes the coffee?' he suggested as he turned his horse.

'You don't frighten me,' she called back, laughing.

She went ahead, but Tiago caught up with her easily and for a few strides they rode side by side. But he couldn't resist taking the lead. She let him go, just for the sheer pleasure of watching him with one hand on the reins and his hips working effortlessly to a lazy rhythm. Arousal lodged deep inside her at the sight of him, and she finally admitted to herself that Friday couldn't come quickly enough.

Clattering into the yard after him, she dismounted. Tiago's dark eyes were wicked, and there was a smile on his lips as she started untacking her pony. 'Make sure you sleep tonight. There won't be much sleeping on Friday.'

Hefting his tack, he walked past her.

She stilled with her hand resting on the saddle. She had to take a deep breath before she could continue. She wanted him. His deep, husky voice had sent heat coursing through her. She wanted to marry Tiago. Worse, she wanted to live with him and share his life. But every time that thought slipped through she had to remind herself that theirs was a marriage of convenience, with a time limit of one year. Any fantasies on her part were just that: fantasies.

It seemed surreal to be standing in the middle of a dance floor at Tiago's side. They were at the gauchos' party and he was calling for silence with his arms raised.

Everything was moving at breakneck speed. In two days they would be married.

So? What was her problem? The wedding on Friday was no surprise, so why the jitters?

She was decked out in her one and only dress, with her hair neatly tied back and hardly any make-up, trying to make a good impression. She was at ease around these people in the corral, or in the kitchen, but here, at Tiago's side, it all seemed so improbable. He was like a god to them, and she had just sprung out of nowhere. What must they think?

Never mind what anyone thought—for the sake of these people she had to make a go of this. Why cause problems when Tiago had worked so hard to save the ranch?

'Danny?'

Tiago's voice held a note of command and her eyes

flashed open. How could she live with this man, love him, and then leave him without a backward glance?

She couldn't.

Glancing round the smiling faces, she felt like the worst kind of confidence trickster. The only way she could get through this was by concentrating on the fact that her marriage to Tiago would secure the future of everyone here. Meanwhile, Brazil's most eligible bachelor—the man she adored—was announcing their wedding to cries of excitement from the crowd.

'I realise that Danny will have already told some of you, and you may think that this has all happened at the speed of light, but Danny and I have known each other for quite some time, and recently our friendship has turned into something more.'

Everyone cheered at this romantic interpretation of their cold-blooded contract, and when Tiago turned to look at her she could almost believe it too.

Putting his arm around her shoulder, he led her out of the spotlight to a crescendo of cheers, and then his men distracted him, coming up to shake his hand, while the women and children of the ranch clustered around Danny.

'And now I have a special gift for my bride,' he announced.

Taking hold of her hand, he led her through the crowd to the space beyond the dance floor.

'Another gift?' Danny stared up into Tiago's rugged face. 'You don't have to.'

'But I want to.'

His sharp whistle of command caused a commotion in the crowd, and everyone fell back at the sound of thundering hooves. Danny gasped as the young colt galloped towards them.

'Is there anything else you'd rather have?'

'Nothing,' she said. 'But—'

'Then accept him and be gracious,' Tiago advised. 'You have to think like a businesswoman now, Danny. This colt will be a valuable stud one day.'

It would have been better if she have thought like a businesswoman from the start, Danny reflected, stunned by Tiago's gift. Her marriage was an advantageous merger for them both, nothing more—just as this young colt, Firefly, was an advantageous acquisition.

'Thank you.' She moved quickly to the young horse's head, to soothe him and to speak to him gently, wanting him to focus on her and be calm, rather than focus on the noisy crowd.

'I'm glad he gives you pleasure.'

'There's nothing you could have given me that I would treasure more.' Nestling her face against the colt's warm neck, she breathed in the familiar scent and wished, just for a moment, that one day she would ride him with Tiago at her side.

The colt was led away to a round of appreciative applause. Everyone on the ranch understood the significance of such a gift. It was a pledge from Tiago to his people that this marriage would be good for them.

But they didn't know the ins and outs of it, Danny fretted as she smiled to show that she couldn't have been happier with her gift. There could be no certainties in life, she told herself firmly as Tiago spoke to some of the men. Surely every bride-to-be felt this way—that to be so happy must come at a cost?

'It's official, Danny.'

She tried to close her heart to Tiago, but when he took hold of her hands to draw her close she failed miserably. Even when he dipped his head to kiss her she suspected it was for the sake of the crowd.

'We've made everyone happy tonight,' he said.

'Yes,' she agreed.

Sensing her unease, Tiago led her out of the crowd. 'Is that all you have to say?'

He had every right to expect her to be bouncing with happiness after his announcement of their engagement, the upcoming wedding, and now his wonderful gift, but she couldn't fake it.

Why must she always pick holes in perfection? Why wouldn't the fairytale work for her?

He ground his jaw, seeing the tension in Danny's back as she walked away with a group of women who were keen to help her organise their wedding. Nothing must go wrong now. His lawyers were standing by. Full ownership of the ranch was a matter of hours away.

He was as tense as he had ever been, Tiago realised as a group of his fellow gauchos encouraged him to stay and spend the night celebrating with them. His determination to build on what he'd started with these people had never been stronger than it was today.

And Danny?

Deus! A million things could go wrong between now and their wedding day. Suddenly Friday seemed an eternity away.

This could work, Danny thought on Thursday morning as she waved goodbye to the women who had helped her to design the menu for their wedding banquet. She had left them late last night, after discussing plans for the wedding, and had felt much calmer after spending time with them. She had slept well for the first time in ages.

Maybe because there had had been no sign of Tiago, she thought now with amusement, as he stood at her side in the middle of the courtyard, supposedly survey-ing the decorations when he was clearly itching to go on his morning ride.

'Happy?' Tiago asked as the lively group trooped home.

'Yes,' Danny said. 'I am now I know that this is the type of wedding we're having. I honestly couldn't think of anything better.'

'Everyone wants to help because they think a lot of you.'

'I hope that's true.'

'Didn't I tell you everything would be all right?'

'Yes,' she murmured, wondering if once they were married she'd even see him.

It was too late to worry about that now, Danny con-cluded, heading for the house as Tiago turned for the stables—or so she thought.

She hadn't realised but he was coming after her, and she exclaimed with surprise.

'Not long now.' He cupped her chin, and his eyes blazed into her own. 'Is there anything that could make this better for you, *chica*?'

If you loved me, she thought, *that would make it bet-ter. If this marriage of ours were not a sham, that would make it better still.*

'Your friends from Rottingdean?' he suggested.

'Lizzie and Chico are still on honeymoon, and with Hamish and Annie in charge of the house in their ab-sence—'

'What about your mother?'

'If you can find her.' Danny's mouth twisted with re-gret. 'I'm afraid I don't even know where she is. I keep trying to contact her, but—'

'She's in the South of France,' Tiago revealed, shock-ing her.

'What's she doing there?'

'Spending the last of the money you sent her, I imagine.'

'Did you speak to her?' she asked urgently.

Hope soared inside her. She'd always been a dream-weaver, and if there was the slightest chance she could speak to her mother, make her understand, reassure her about this marriage...

'Yes. I've spoken to her,' he confirmed. 'I wanted everything to be perfect for you—or as perfect as it can be. You're doing so much for me, Danny. I don't think you even realise what you're doing. I would have flown your mother out here for the wedding, but there are some things even I can't control.'

'What did she say to you?' She couldn't hide her eagerness. 'Did she get my messages?'

'She got all of them, apparently.'

Tiago's grim look warned her to be brave.

'What did she say?'

'She said they were blocking up her phone, and could you please stop?'

CHAPTER NINE

'Oh.' Danny's voice was flat. The shock of what Tiago had told her cut deep. She couldn't blame him for his candour after she'd pressed him for an answer. She guessed he'd thought a clean cut would be the best. The news that her mother wasn't interested in Danny was old, but it hurt all the same. The fact that her mother didn't even care that she was getting married was brutal.

'You tried, Danny. At least you tried.'

Yes, she was certainly a trier, Danny reflected dryly. How stupid she felt now, imagining her mother would want to wish her well.

'I can't honestly say I expected her to be here for the wedding,' she admitted, pinning a smile to her face.

She glanced up to find Tiago staring down at her with concern. Maybe she was wrong about him. Maybe he did have feelings but, having spent a lifetime hiding them, now found them impossible to express.

'Don't feel sorry for me, Tiago. I'm not a child.'

'Maybe not,' he agreed, 'but my people show you more affection than your own mother. If she had been born with a title, and then squandered an old man's fortune, I would say that your mother and mine must have been twins.'

The bitterness in his voice told her that Tiago had experience of loving someone and being rejected. She knew that that could lead down one of two roads: the road *she* trod, where she never stopped trying, or the road Tiago had taken, where he simply turned his back. It was another thought to unsettle her.

'I can't bear to see you hurt like this,' he raged.

'I'm not hurt. I'm—'

'Accustomed to it?' he spat out. 'Why *should* you be accustomed to it? This is wrong, Danny. You should cut her out of your life.'

'She's my mother. I can't.'

'She's no mother to you.'

With an impatient gesture, Tiago ground his jaw, but thankfully said nothing more on the subject.

'Don't worry,' he said at last. 'Everyone on the ranch will be here to cheer you on.'

'And that's all that matters,' she said with conviction.

She only had to remember how touched she'd been when a selection of treasured veils and wedding dresses had been brought out of lavender-scented storage for her to choose from to know how much Tiago's people meant to her.

'They're your people now, Danny,' he said, reading her.

'*Our* people.'

That thought made her feel strong. Whatever happened in the future, the bond she was building here with the people of Fazenda Santos would support her as surely as any strong family could.

'They've done so much in the short time they've known me to make me feel welcome,' she said, glancing round the courtyard, which was already dressed for the wedding, 'and I'm honoured to have been accepted here.'

'You'll be happy. I'll make sure of it,' he said.

But when Tiago put his arm around her shoulders and drew her close she thought, *Yes, but for just one year.*

She was certain that Tiago would do his best to make her time in Brazil trouble-free. It wasn't in his interest to do otherwise. He would never risk this marriage of convenience being challenged by anyone.

'One last drink before we part?' he suggested.

'Why not?' She smiled.

Tomorrow was their wedding day. It hardly seemed possible. Closing her eyes briefly, she drank in his strength, wishing with all her heart that they were a normal couple, with a normal relationship. But what *was* normal? Could any couple enter into marriage with complete certainty?

Shaking off her doubts, she walked with him towards the outdoor area at the back of the ranch house, where Tiago loved to stand and look out across his property. She reminded herself that for some married couples it wasn't even possible to guarantee a happy year.

The hunter had become the protector. His cold-blooded plan to marry Danny at all costs had been brought to its knees by the way she was treated by her mother. No one should be treated like that. Hot blood surged through his veins as Danny stood beside him. There was anger, and there was lust—and something else he refused to name. Twenty-four hours ago he had held her in his arms—and that seemed too long.

Glancing down, he saw how pale she was. The conversation he'd had with her about her mother had hit her hard. He should have found some gentler way to break it to her. He shouldn't have been surprised by her resilience, but he was. He poured her a drink—orange juice, as she'd requested. She was determined to keep a clear head, he concluded, quelling his disappointment at the thought that temptation would have to be resisted for another night.

'Why are you smiling?' she asked him when he took the empty glass from her hand.

'You're wearing a dress, and I don't think I've ever seen your legs before.'

'Liar. You saw me at the wedding in a bridesmaid's dress.'

'Which trailed around your ankles.' He tipped the neck of his bottle of beer in Danny's direction.

She shook her head. 'It did not trail.' And then she said, 'Shall we drink a toast to your grandfather?'

'My grandfather? I'm surprised you're even thinking about him.'

'Why wouldn't I? We wouldn't be here without him,' she pointed out.

His lips pressed down with amusement as he shook his head. She was right. His grandfather might have done a lot of things he disagreed with, but he had given Tiago the chance to change his life.

Easing onto one hip, he told her a little more about his history. 'I never imagined my grandfather would deny me full ownership of the ranch, but he was cunning, and he never liked my playboy antics. He said it reminded him too much of my mother—the feckless socialite, as he called her. That's why he constructed his will as he did. He knew how much I loved this place. He knew I wouldn't let the people down.'

'Whatever it took?' Danny observed dryly.

'Whatever it took,' he agreed, meeting her stare head-on. The one thing he would never do was lie to her.

'To your grandfather,' she said softly, chinking her glass against his bottle. 'Manuelo told me your parents were never around, and that when they were they only came here to beg for money from your grandfather. Once they got that, he said they left—sometimes without even seeing you. So what's the sequel to this story, Tiago? I know there must be one, because Manuelo thinks the world of you—as does everyone else on this ranch.'

He was reluctant to get into it, but from the look in her eyes Danny wasn't giving up. 'My grandfather bailed me out of a juvenile correctional facility—said he'd give me a trial on the ranch. He said I could live with him if I worked for the privilege.'

'And you fought him every step of the way?' she guessed.

He didn't deny it. 'I didn't want to work for anyone except myself. And when I saw this place in the middle of nowhere—' He grimaced. 'I didn't feel as I do now about it, that's for sure. It held no appeal for my teen-age self.'

'But you stayed?' she pressed, her eyes filled with concern.

'Yes, because I came to love the people. And now you've met them I'm sure you understand why.'

'I do.' She spoke softly and touched his arm.

He had to pause and hold himself in check for a moment, or he would have responded for sure.

'I try never to be away from them for long,' he went on then. 'Because they and my grandfather opened my eyes to a different way of life—*their* way of life. And I could relate to it—to them. The passion they have for the country and their animals is the same as mine, and as soon as the gauchos discovered I had a way with horses, that was it—I was one of them. It was enough for me for a time, and then—like everyone else when they're growing up—I had to get away. I was desperate to expand my horizons—to explore that other side of me, bequeathed to me by my mother.'

He laughed as he thought about it.

'And then?' Danny asked.

'My grandfather was wise enough to back off and leave me to it.'

'Where did you go?'

'I hitched my wagon to whichever polo player was fashionable at the time.' He shrugged. 'By watching and learning I somehow managed to save up enough from my wages to buy my first pony. She was an old girl, on the point of retirement, but I was eager to try the game myself, and I made a passable polo pony out of her. Thanks to that mare I could take part in at least one chukka during amateur matches, where not every rider owned a string of ponies and we all did the best we could.'

'Which brought your riding skills to the attention of those that mattered?'

'Correct.'

She was standing close enough to touch, and that distracted him for another few moments.

'Eventually I was entrusted with training a few medium-grade ponies.' He cast his mind back to those uncertain days. 'Then my grandfather became ill, but I was having too much of a good time to come home. I should have come. I owe everything I have to him. I just couldn't see it at the time. Now do you understand why I am so committed to this place?'

'Yes,' she said quietly. 'It explains a lot about you.'

'Like why I'm such a selfish bastard?' He laughed.

'Like why you belong here,' Danny argued. 'And why you believe you can never do enough for this ranch or for the people who live here. You think you deserted your grandfather when he needed you most, but he had let you go, knowing you'd come back. He wanted you to see how wide your horizons could be. You haven't let him down, Tiago—anything but.'

'Some of the decisions I've had to make to keep this ranch haven't been easy.'

She shook her head and laughed. 'I think I know that.' She looked into his eyes and hers darkened.

The pain in his groin increased. Taking hold of her wrist, he led her around the side of the house, and with the utmost self-control he held her away from him at the door.

'Goodnight, Danny. The next time I see you will be at our wedding.'

Could there be anything more beautiful than his bride on their wedding day? He couldn't hold back a smile as Danny walked slowly towards him down the petal-strewn aisle. She was coming to join him through packed rows of people whose smiling faces meant the world to him.

The fact that they were fast adopting Danny as one of their own was the icing on the cake for him, but he didn't need anyone to tell him that he'd made a wonderful choice of bride. Danny had so much to offer the ranch and its people. When they were married he hoped she would play an even bigger role, adding the human touch he'd never had time to bring to the ranch.

The outdoor ceremony beneath an archway of flowers passed quickly, in a series of softly spoken words on Danny's part and brisk assertions on his. He would take away a series of sensory memories, together with the relief of being married.

Danny was small and soft and fragrant—and so keyed-up, so alert she was almost trembling. Her close-fitting lace dress was rustling, though she wasn't moving. It rustled when she breathed and her breasts rose above the confining fabric, and it rustled when she turned to him to speak her wedding vows, and through all this they were standing close, but not touching, and that tiny space keeping them apart was charged with electricity.

'You may kiss the bride.'

At last he could breathe freely. He was married. He owned the ranch. The relief of having the caveat in his grandfather's will fulfilled was indescribable. His people sensed it too and cheered wildly, standing to applaud as he cupped Danny's face in his hands. The future security of everyone here was assured now. This was his gift to his guests. He had an aide on hand, waiting to make a copy of the wedding certificate, as well as a courier standing by to deliver a hard copy to the lawyers as soon as this ceremony was over.

This was more romantic than she had dared to hope. Surrounded by fragrant blossoms in front of the registrar, she could feel love swelling all around her. She knew she was doing the right thing. Tiago's steady gaze was all it took to convince her that her doubts before the wedding had been based on nothing more than pre-wedding nerves.

Surely Tiago must feel the magic too? How could he not? Danny wondered as he dipped his head and kissed her. She closed her eyes, knowing she'd never been so happy. Even the cruel barbs in the press couldn't touch her now. She remembered some of them, and smiled as Tiago stared deep into her eyes.

Can a small-town girl rein in a man like Tiago Santos?

Yes, she could.

Does a leopard change his spots?

Yes, he had.

'Will the Playboy be curbed by Miss Whiplash?'

That remark had made her laugh. Nothing mattered now except the fact that Tiago Santos and Danny Cameron were husband and wife. The reporters didn't know him as she did. No one who hadn't seen Tiago Santos on this ranch had seen the real man.

'Well, Senhora Santos, are you ready to start your new life with me?'

'I am.'

'When you look at me like that,' Tiago murmured, 'all I can think about is taking you to bed. Is that bad?'

'I like you bad. Tonight I think I'm going to be very bad too.'

'I'm counting on it,' Tiago assured her.

He excited her. She trembled in an entirely pleasurable way at the thought of their wedding night. She'd asked for this delay, and could hardly believe how long she'd waited—not long in actual terms of this week, but if she counted in her feverish erotic daydreams from that first moment she saw him in Brazil, that was quite a build-up to tonight.

She was about to find out if her imagination was equal to their wedding night. Pleasure thrummed through her at the thought that she might not even be close.

But they had guests to entertain first, Danny remembered as Tiago was distracted by some of his polo-playing friends.

While he was talking she stared at the jewel-encrusted band on her hand, sitting snugly next to the enormous diamond engagement ring. How incongruous they looked on her work-worn hands. Silk purse and sow's ear came to mind.

She flashed a glance at Tiago—blisteringly hot, unreasonably handsome, sleekly tailored and unimaginably successful—and in spite of all the encouragement she'd been giving herself before the wedding she shrank a little inside her beautiful borrowed wedding dress.

The wedding party might have been last-minute but, as he had expected, everyone had pulled together to make it special. It was the best party he'd been to in a long time, and every time he looked at his bride he knew he'd made a good choice.

His groin was straining, begging for him to do something about it, but he was beginning to enjoy the agony— and he wanted to show off his beautiful wife. So many people were waiting to congratulate them that any chance of their being alone was slim, at least for now, but hearing tributes from the heart from his people made it easy to stay.

'It's thrilling to feel part of such a wonderful extended family,' Danny told him. 'I feel closer than ever to this ranch.'

Covering her hand with his, he linked their fingers. 'Are you frustrated?'

Her eyes cleared as she took his meaning, and then she held his gaze and smiled. 'Of course I am.'

Heat swept over him. He wanted her *now*.

'Do you think me too obvious? Too unsophisticated?'

'No. I think you're a normal healthy woman, with a normal healthy appetite.'

He smiled into her eyes, but she pulled back.

'*Deus*, Danny. You look as if I have you by the throat. You can't be frightened of your wedding night?'

'I'm not,' she said, not entirely convincingly.

Putting his arm around her shoulder, he stared into her eyes. 'So if it isn't that, what is it?' He thought of Pintos and the pain she'd suffered. 'You *do* know I'd never hurt you, don't you?'

She laughed—a little sadly, he thought. 'Of course I do. At least not for a year,' she joked, and was soon smiling again.

'You will be secure for the rest of your life,' he reminded her. 'I promise you, Danny, I'll never forget what you've done for me. You will never need to worry again.'

Her eyes clouded. 'Do we have to talk about that now?'

'No.' He slanted a smile. 'What would you rather talk about, *chica*?'

Would Tiago ever understand that this wasn't about the money? Or that she hurt because they had not once said they loved each other? But why should they? It wouldn't be right. It wouldn't be appropriate. She might love Tiago, but even on their wedding day it wouldn't be right to tell him how she felt. They had a contract—nothing more. She had payment. He had the ranch. This wasn't about love. This wedding was for public consumption, to put a seal of approval on the secret they held between them that would bind them together for no more than a year.

She moved restlessly, and was rewarded by the lift of his ebony brow. It didn't help her composure when she wanted him so badly in every way there was. She ached to be held in his arms and made love to in every sense. Their faces were so close she could see the glint of tiger-gold in his eyes, and that look...that darkening slumberous look.

'Is there anything I can do to help you?' he murmured, teasing her into an even higher state of arousal with those words. 'Bearing in mind that we may be here for some time...?'

CHAPTER TEN

HER BODY PULSED with need while her mind screamed at her to hold back. 'Help me with what?' She frowned, pretending ignorance—anything rather than give way to Tiago and be lost.

He shared none of her inhibitions. 'Help you with that ache,' he said frankly, holding her gaze.

'I'm not sure what ache you're talking about.'

'Think back to the jet.'

'Here?'

Now he had shocked her. She was no prude, but what had happened between them in Tiago's bedroom on his private jet couldn't possibly happen here at their wedding party.

His expression grew darker. 'No one will notice,' he said, with the hint of a smile.

'You *are* joking?' Danny answered, looking around the room.

They were somewhat secluded from the other guests, but might be interrupted at any time. The idea was both shocking and thrilling for Danny.

'Am I?' He was already moving her skirts aside. 'Stop finding reasons not to, and concentrate on why you should.' His mouth was still curving wickedly—and so confidently. 'Look at me, Danny,' he murmured. 'Just keep looking at me, and let me do the rest...'

She gasped as his hand found her. It felt so warm and big and strong and sure as he cupped her. Tiago was so wicked, but she couldn't stop herself edging forward just a little to help him. She was already lost, her senses in chaos, and her body was tuned to his smallest touch. She had been well trained by Tiago on the flight over, to respond to pleasure this way, and she instantly concentrated on that one place to the exclusion of everything else.

The noise of the party, the chatter and laughter of their guests, even the band playing loudly, couldn't compete with the thundering of her heart or the rasp of her breathing as Tiago's lightest touch brought wave after wave of pleasure washing over her.

'Tell me to stop if you want to,' he said in a matter-of-fact tone as she lost it completely.

She could only answer him with a soft groan when the fiercest waves had subsided—and then he began to move his hand with more intent. She sucked in a sharp breath as his fingers worked their magic. Tiago knew just what to do, what she liked, and how to administer pleasure in a leisurely fashion, so she could savour every moment and make it last.

His fingers were so sensitive to her needs, so skilful as they went about their work. At first he avoided the place where she needed him most, and teasing her this way made her mad for him. By moving a little further forward in her chair she managed to increase the pressure of his hand, and then he passed his forefinger lightly over her straining clitoris until she gasped—only to moan with disappointment when he pulled away.

'Not for long, *chica*,' he whispered, his breath warm against her face.

His hand quickly found the ribbons holding her bridal thong in place. It was a wisp of lace, nothing more, but he took his time unlooping the bow; unwrapping her slowly, like the revealing of a gift he was in no mood to rush.

'Move to the very edge of the chair,' he instructed, 'and lean back.'

She was quick to do as he said, her excitement intensified by the risk involved as their guests milled all around them.

'There's so much noise no one will notice what you do, but try not to cry out too loudly,' Tiago advised. 'Now, open your legs a little wider for me.'

She opened them as wide as she could, wanting that plump, needy place to be the centre of his universe.

'Oh, yes...'

Excited by the risk, and by the promise in Tiago's lazy tone, she rested back and waited.

'Relax... Enjoy...' he murmured, as if she needed prompting. 'Just leave everything to me.'

Oh, she would... She *would*...

'Ah...' The touch of his slightly roughened finger-pad was exquisite.

'I'll catch you when you fall,' he promised. 'Just keep looking into my eyes and I'll tell you when.'

'You'll *know*?' she somehow managed to gasp out.

'I'll know.'

'Oh...' She grabbed a breath and concentrated.

Tiago's finger was circling repeatedly, maintaining just the right amount of friction... 'Wide,' he reminded her, pressing her legs apart. 'And keep looking at me.'

She grabbed a shuddering breath. 'I'm not sure how long I can hold on...' Her eyes widened as she stared at him.

'I know,' he soothed.

Those eyes—that touch...

She whimpered as he began to rub faster, and with just the right pressure. 'I can't—'

'Then don't,' he said in a different tone. 'Let go now...'

Tiago drowned her cries of pleasure against his chest and held her firmly as she lost control.

'And that's just the start of our wedding night,' he promised, smiling down at her as she sank into his arms.

He strolled back with Danny to the house, making painfully slow progress as everyone who hadn't yet congratulated them seized their chance. He welcomed their good wishes, telling himself that if control was good for him it was even better for Danny.

The women on the ranch had asked him if they could prepare a scented bath for her, and he had agreed, hoping this would please and reassure her. He wouldn't risk anything going wrong now—not with so many witnesses on the ranch. His representative had already left to take the marriage certificate to the lawyers. The ranch was his, thanks to Danny.

When they reached the door he swept her into his arms and carried her across the threshold.

'I didn't know if you would do that,' she said, laughing up at him, her face alive with happiness as he lowered her to her feet

'I don't forget anything where you're concerned. Would you like me to help you out of your dress?'

Suddenly, she was shy. 'If you could just unbutton it for me, please?'

Her voice was tight with nerves.

'Whatever you want.'

This wasn't the Danny he had enjoyed getting to know all over again—the girl who had already become an essential cog in the wheel that was Fazenda Santos. This was a girl who still harboured doubts and it was up to him to resolve them.

He had barely unfastened the last button when she picked up her skirts and fled up the stairs.

'First on the right,' he called after her. 'The women have made a surprise for you.'

She paused and turned, hovering on the stairs. 'Aren't you coming up?'

'Of course I am. This is our wedding night.'

Their eyes locked for a moment, and then she carried on, running to the first floor, while he held back. She reminded him of a wild pony—trapped and uncertain in its new circumstances.

'Take your time...relax,' he called up the stairs.

She disappeared out of sight without answering him.

The silence was heavy in the hall. Maybe that was why the shadow of doubt fell over him. He had been so certain that for this one year he could make Danny happy, and that when that year was over she would have everything she could possibly need and he would be free. But she was proving as elusive as a wisp of smoke that kept slipping through his fingers, which left him in the unique position of wondering if he could hold her for as long as a year.

Danny exclaimed with pleasure when she walked into the bathroom. The women had gone to so much trouble for her, with scented candles and fresh flowers strewn everywhere. She turned full circle, knowing that she didn't deserve this. How could she, when her marriage was a charade? But to waste their preparations for her would be throwing their generosity back in their faces.

Releasing the hem of her dress, she let it fall to the floor and stepped out of it. Climbing into the bath, she sank into the warm, sudsy water and lay back, closing her eyes. She could hear a shower running somewhere close by. When it stopped she pictured Tiago stepping out, grabbing a towel and winding it around his body. She waited a few more seconds and then sat up.

Just in time. The door opened and he was there. Just as she had imagined, his powerful torso was naked, while his body was gleaming and barely dry.

'You're lucky,' he said, smiling as he glanced around her fairy dell. 'The women have really gone to town for you.'

Her heart beat faster as he strolled deeper into the room. He picked up a towel, unfolded it and held it out. She climbed out of the bath, naked and transfixed by his eyes. She had no doubts left. This had nothing to do with the contract. This was what she wanted.

Tiago wrapped her in a towel and lifted her into his arms. He carried her into his bedroom and laid her down on the bed. Unlooping the towel from his waist, he let it drop. The room was silent apart from her breathing. The bed yielded to his weight with a sigh.

His muscles were formidable close up. She had never seen him naked before. His skin was deeply tanned to a rich bronze, and scarred from a lifetime of taking riding to the limits—maybe scarred from his youth too, she remembered, knowing he'd been wild.

She traced his tattoos, those brutal reminders of the Thunderbolts polo team, with an exclamation mark for emphasis—intended, no doubt, to strike fear into the team's opponents. His stubble was thick, his hair was thick too, and his gold earring glinted in the light. He was like no man she'd ever seen before. He was the perfect barbarian. And he was *her* barbarian.

'Slowly, *chica*,' he advised as she pressed against him. 'I'm big and you're small.'

'No...' She smiled cheekily up at him.

But, yes, he *was* big—and she was small by comparison and she loved that. She loved the weight of his erection pressing against her thigh, and exclaimed softly when his hand found her.

'Are you surprised?' she murmured, when he raised a brow at how ready she was.

'Not surprised,' he growled as he moved over her, to start teasing her with his velvet-smooth tip.

'You can't do that,' she complained. 'You can't tease me like that.'

'Really?' He smiled faintly. 'I think you'll find I can.'

A cry escaped her when he probed deeper, but he took his time and waited until he'd built her confidence. Then he moved a little more, a little deeper, stretching her beyond imagining, but his knowing fingers made her forget the shock of it.

'Do you want me?'

'You know I do,' she forced out shakily

'Deep?'

'Yes,' she confirmed.

'Firmly?' Tiago suggested, smiling, his lips brushing hers.

'Please...'

'Now?'

She cried out with pleasure as this big man, who looked so brutal but was so careful with her, took her smoothly until he was lodged deep. Then he rested, giving her a chance to recover from the invasion and catch her breath. She hung on to him, her hands clutching as she gasped with excitement. And then he cupped her buttocks, and that felt so good. It turned her on to think of those big, strong hands controlling her. He lifted her onto him and began to move with regular, dependable strokes, until she was whimpering in time with every one.

She reached her climax fast—too fast—and lost control with a throaty scream of shock. And then she was all melting, soaring, gliding on thunderclaps of sensation.

'More?' Tiago suggested when she was finally reduced to astonished sobs.

'Please...' She only needed that one word in her vocabulary, Danny concluded as she stared into Tiago's eyes.

She pressed her mouth against his shoulder as he began to move again, faster now. She clung on tightly as the primal imperative to move with him, to work with him, claimed her.

'Let me pleasure you,' he encouraged huskily, opening her legs wider still.

'Yes...' she agreed. This was everything she had ever wanted, and it thrilled her all the more to know that Tiago needed her too.

She exclaimed with disappointment when he withdrew, and then laughed when she realised that he was teasing her. When he sank deep again she moaned and pressed her mouth against his neck.

'More?'

'As much as you can give me?' she suggested. Her whole world was sensation now, and he had centred it in that one place.

He thrust deep and pulled out, then thrust deep again. Her heart cried out to him to give her everything, to find his release. Grabbing hold of his buttocks, so firm and muscular, she moved with him. She was demanding now, claiming her mate and moving as strongly as he was with every stroke. They were both ravenous for this, and she could be as fierce as Tiago.

It was only a matter of moments before she felt the pressure building again and, seeing the mist of pleasure reflected in Tiago's eyes, she knew he was close too.

'I'll tell you when,' he cautioned.

'Now,' she said fiercely.

He could do nothing to stop her—to stop himself—as she tightened her muscles around him. They were both lost, both swept up in a fire storm of sensation, and when she found release he did too.

If only she hadn't read the screen on Tiago's computer. She had come downstairs for two glasses of water while Tiago was in the shower, and she hadn't been able to wait to get back to bed. But now she was squatting on the kitchen floor with her arms over her head, pressing—pressing hard—as she tried to make the words on the screen go away.

If she hadn't come down to the kitchen she wouldn't have nudged his computer and the screen wouldn't have flashed on. It was too late now. She'd seen it. And, short minutes after crying with happiness, she had tears of desperation pouring down her face.

She never learned. She always trusted. She always hoped for the best. And now she was a ridiculous bride in a skimpy outfit that one of the young girls had left out for her to wear on her wedding night. The decorated bathroom, with its candles and scent bottles and flowers, had been wasted on her. The women on the ranch had wanted her to feel like a treasured bride, when in fact she was a complete idiot.

Burying her head again, she hugged it harder. But the words on the screen still flashed in front of her eyes.

'You will never hear anything good about yourself if you eavesdrop, Danny,' her grandmother had used to say.

And you wouldn't read anything good about yourself either—as she had just discovered. Tiago had been in the middle of writing an email back to Lizzie when he had broken off—presumably because the gauchos had arrived to escort him to their wedding. And once she had started reading the screen she hadn't been able to stop. She had even scrolled back to read the rest of Lizzie's messages.

It had been about then that she had ended up on the floor. Her legs must have given way as her world had shattered.

It was all lies. Tiago had lied to her by omission.

The subject line on Lizzie's email had been enough without the rest: Chico told me. That sounded so accusatory. What could Chico possibly have told Lizzie to make Danny's best friend so angry?

Reading on, she'd found out.

I know you'll stop at nothing to secure the ranch, because I know *you*, Tiago, but your plan smacks of desperation to me. And if you hurt her—if you force Danny to do anything she doesn't want to do—you might be Chico's friend, but I swear I'll never forgive you.

Danny's *my* friend, and I *will* protect her. You can't marry someone simply because you need a wife and a baby fast. When I challenged Chico about it he said you would keep the child, but not the mother. How *could* you, Tiago? I refuse to believe my friend would agree to this unless you've lied to her—and when she finds out her heart will be broken again.

Please send her home. The work on the roof is nearly finished, so the house is safe to live in, and we'll be back from honeymoon soon. Please tell Danny she always has a home here—

Tiago would keep her baby?

Danny shook her head in desperation. It wasn't so much the fact that Lizzie obviously believed Danny's marriage to Tiago was doomed but the thought of having her child taken from her that had stopped her in her tracks.

Tiago had never mentioned anything about a baby. Even when she had confronted him about the possibility of their having a child he had shrugged it off. No system of birth control was absolutely reliable, and they had used none today, but if Tiago thought he could take her child away from her—he didn't know her at all. She would fight to defend her child to her dying breath.

What was *wrong* with him? The terms of his grandfather's will had been unreasonable. Tiago had acknowledged that. His grandfather had wanted him to found a dynasty that carried his name, but they had both agreed how outdated that was.

Saving the ranch was something she could support—but tearing a child from its mother?

A chill of dread swept over her. Tiago believed he had to comply exactly with the terms of his grandfather's will or risk losing everything: the community he'd built, the wonderful people... Everything he cared about would be destroyed. And she had entered into this arrangement with her eyes wide open. But did an unborn child deserve to be a pawn in their game?

It wasn't going to happen. She wouldn't *let* it happen. She couldn't change him. She had to get that through her head. Tiago's childhood experience had been with utterly selfish parents and he'd built a carapace of steel around his heart. *Her* past had made her determined to survive anything—and she would survive this.

CHAPTER ELEVEN

'DANNY?'

She could hear him coming down the stairs, and his purposeful stride heading towards the kitchen. She was on her feet, leaning over the kitchen counter with her arms braced and her fists planted. She didn't move when he came into the room. She couldn't bear to look at him. She didn't respond in any way.

'Are you okay? Danny—what's wrong?'

Tiago was at her side in moments, still warm and damp from the shower. She could smell soap on him, she registered numbly as she pushed his hand away.

She stepped to one side, but he stood in front of her.

'Speak to me, Danny.' Dipping his head, Tiago searched her eyes.

She turned her face away. 'I think it's better if I don't talk now.'

He straightened up. 'What do you mean?'

'I'm angry, Tiago, and I don't want to say anything in the heat of the moment to make it worse.'

'To make what worse?' he demanded. Raking his hair, he shook his head impatiently. 'I'm in the dark, here. Can you help me?'

Danny didn't know if she could. 'I owe you an apology.'

'What are you *talking* about?' Tiago flared.

'I read your email. I know I shouldn't have, but I came to get us both some water and I nudged your laptop by mistake. The screen flashed on and I read it. I read your exchanges with Lizzie.'

A shiver gripped her as Tiago swore softly under his breath.

'Can you explain them?' she asked quietly. 'Can you tell me why you didn't think to tell me that a baby was part of our deal?'

'You must have known—'

'That there was a possibility I could have a child? Of course I knew. I tried to discuss it with you, but you brushed it off.'

'I didn't brush it off,' he defended.

'Well, let me tell you this, so there can be no misunderstanding. If I'm lucky enough to have a child, no one on this earth is going to rip that child from my arms.'

'Let me explain—'

'You're going to explain *now*?' She shook her head. 'It's too late. Don't you see that? I don't think you were ever going to tell me, Tiago. I think you hoped nature would take its course and that it wouldn't be necessary to tell me that a baby was part of the deal. And then— and I can't imagine how you came to *this* conclusion— you must have thought I'd be content to leave with my money and without my baby at the end of our allotted year. How could you think that, Tiago? Why didn't you say something? Didn't you think I was strong enough to hear the truth?'

'That rubbish in my grandfather's will means nothing. It would never stand up in law.'

'But it must have crossed your mind at some point that it might be a good idea, or why would Chico have mentioned it to Lizzie? Come on, Tiago—say something to make me believe I've misread this, that I've misunderstood your intentions. *Please!*'

'It was a talking point and nothing more.'

'A *talking point*?'

'It was careless talk with Chico about a ridiculous demand by my grandfather that I had no intention of pursuing.'

'Really? Careless talk?' Firming her lips angrily, she shook her head. 'Would that be "careless talk" back in the days when you were a playboy? Let me see—how many days ago would that be? And I'm supposed to believe you've changed?' She made a contemptuous sound.

'Danny, I *have* changed.'

'Have you, Tiago?'

'You've changed me.'

'I'm supposed to believe that, am I?'

'I would have told you everything—but not today. I didn't want to spoil our wedding day.'

'But you *have* spoiled it. You might as well tell me everything now.'

She twirled the fabulous engagement ring and the jewelled wedding band next to it round and round her finger, until the rings threatened to cut into her skin.

'Shall I summarise for you?' she suggested, when Tiago said nothing. 'You bought me, and you think you've bought any baby I might have too. That's why you gave me so much money. I understand now. It all makes sense. They do it in supermarkets—buy one, get one free.'

'Danny—'

'Well, how would *you* put it?' she flared, her shoulders braced, ready to confront him. 'To add insult to injury, you not only transferred an obscene amount of money into my bank account, you tried to pretend our relationship was close to normal with gifts—these rings and that fabulous horse. And to make things even worse I gave *you* gifts—chief amongst which was my heart.'

Almost crying from all the furious emotion inside her, she snatched off the rings and threw them across the counter at him.

'And when I get home I'll be transferring your money back too.'

Tiago snapped alert. 'What are you talking about? When you get home?'

'You can't expect me to stay *now*?'

'I *do* expect you to stay. Of course I do.' His expression grew fierce. 'You're my wife. Where else would you be but with me?' When she laughed incredulously he insisted, 'Come with me, Danny. Come with me now and let me explain.'

'Explain?' She snatched her arm from his grasp. 'I always *knew* this was wrong. Anything you have to say to me can be said right here, right now.'

'This wasn't meant to happen.'

'I'm sure it wasn't,' she agreed.

With an impatient sound, Tiago raked his hair. 'Not tonight—'

'Not ever, I'm guessing.'

'You're wrong, Danny. I know this sounds bad—'

'Bad?' she said over him. 'It doesn't just sound bad—it *is* bad. I'm an adult, Tiago, quite capable of making my own decisions, but it would have helped if I'd known *all* the facts before I agreed to this marriage deal. Now let's be clear. I will not involve an innocent child in this. I can't get past that. Any arrangement we might have had is over. I'm going home.'

She held his blazing stare unflinching, certain that neither of them had expected their marriage to end on their wedding night. She was equally sure that Tiago had never seen her like this before—so cold, so determined, the equal of him. But her childhood hadn't been so very different from his, and she could switch off *her* feelings too.

'If you won't allow me to explain, at least let me get you a robe.'

'Oh, *please*,' she exploded. 'Don't pretend you're concerned about my appearance *now*.'

'But I *am* concerned about you,' Tiago insisted, in a much more collected tone.

He had realised she was serious about leaving him, Danny guessed as she gazed down at her flimsy outfit. It was so inappropriate for what was happening, and it upset her to think that it had been so carefully chosen for her by a young girl who had wanted nothing but the best for Tiago's bride.

'Do I need to be more suitably dressed when you explain your way out of this?' she suggested bitterly.

'For God's sake, Danny— If you'd just listen to me.'

'I have been listening to you. I've heard everything you've said. It's what you haven't said that's upset me. You've upset Lizzie—and on her honeymoon too. I shouldn't have had to read those things, Tiago. I believed you. I trusted you.'

Moving past him, she snatched his riding jacket down from the hook on the back of the door and pulled it on. It drowned her, but the jacket served its purpose in that it covered her completely.

'You've always been my number one concern, Danny.'

'Save it,' she said coldly. 'I suppose it was only a matter of you choosing the right time to explain?'

'As a matter of fact, it was,' he agreed. 'Husbands and wives talk. I did say those things to Chico, but that was when I was still formulating a plan. Of course I was going to tell you. I knew there was a risk Lizzie might say something, and I knew it was up to me to reassure you that my grandfather's demands were, and are, completely unacceptable.'

'And when would you have done that, Tiago? In the delivery ward? Or one year from today when our contract was at an end?' She shook her head in despair. 'What type of woman do you think I am?'

'It's precisely because of the type of woman you are that I married you. Yes, this started out as a business deal, but you mean so much more to me than that.'

'Lucky me,' she scoffed. 'And now I suppose you *love* me?' She raised a brow. 'Is that what you're saying?'

'Yes, I do,' Tiago admitted quietly.

'How convenient. Let me tell you something, Tiago. There can be no love without trust. And you've destroyed my trust completely. I don't think you have a clue what love is. I think you've shut yourself off from feelings for so long you'll never understand.'

'I didn't want to hurt you.'

'So you were going to sit me down like a little girl to explain? How patronising. And I thought we entered this marriage as equals.'

'We *are* equals.'

'But some are more equal than others, it seems to me,' she said coldly. 'I was a convenient bride. I get that. But don't think any child of mine is going to be a convenient baby.'

'I've never thought that and I never will.' He blocked her way out of the kitchen. 'There is no small print in our contract that you don't know about. There was talk in my grandfather's will of a child, but that was all part of his delusion and cannot be upheld in law.'

'How disappointing for you.'

'Don't,' he said. 'Please don't be bitter and angry. You never used to be like this—'

'You mean I used to be a mug?'

'No!' Tiago exclaimed.

'Just unlucky, then?' she said. 'Maybe I could have swallowed this too, if you hadn't stirred my maternal instincts—but you have. I fell in love with you, Tiago. That was my mistake. I thought this was going to be the best night of my life—not the worst. And, worst of all, I thought I could change you.'

'You *have* changed me.'

'Have I, Tiago?' Drawing in a shaking breath, she lifted her head to look at him. 'Why can't polo players ever be straight with a woman? Are you all too busy and important to consider the feelings of your fellow human beings? Do we exist only for your convenience?'

'If you're referring to Pintos, I'll take that—because I should have been straight with you from the start. But I was trying to protect you, Danny, and I got it wrong. I would have done anything to protect you. Nothing you've read on that screen suggests that I agree with my grandfather. It's old talk. And he can't enforce his demands from the grave. Nor would I allow him to if he were alive today. And in spite of what you must think of him he wasn't a bad man. He'd just fought so hard for what he had, and he'd lost it once. He couldn't bear to lose it again.'

With an exhausted gesture, he shook his head.

'All I can say is that I wish those emails had never been sent, because then I could reassure you. But, whatever you think of me now, I will always protect you. Maybe I went too far this time, but that's only because I love you.'

'You love me? You don't even know the meaning of the word.'

'Stop it, Danny—this is your insecurity. You're not so different from me. We can work this out.'

'Can we? Why drag it out for a year, Tiago? You have the ranch. My job is done. Why keep up the pretence any longer?'

'Because I love you. Because I'm happier than I've ever been.'

'I don't know what to think any more,' Danny admitted. 'I feel as if every time I put down foundations something comes along to shake them loose.'

'Not this time—I promise you,' Tiago insisted fiercely. 'That's your past talking. Just because your mother's never been there for you. That's not me—that's not now.'

Drawing his jacket tightly around her shoulders, she shook her head. 'I can't give you the answer you want. I'm sorry, Tiago. Maybe it *is* my past getting in the way, but I need time to think this through.'

'Danny—'

'Please…' She backed away. 'I need space to think, and I can't think when I'm close to you.'

He slept the rest of the night in the guest bedroom, while Danny slept in his room. He couldn't say he blamed her for doubting him. A lifetime of blanking out his feelings hadn't helped him to handle the situation better. He could have dealt with Danny angry and hot-tempered more easily, but when she'd turned cold, had spoken to him so bleakly, he had known she was right. The past had a lot to answer for, and she did need time.

But he wasn't ready to give up. Swinging out of bed, he showered and dressed, and then knocked on her door.

'Come on. Get up—we're going riding.'

He wasn't even sure she'd heard him, let alone that she would join him. But she did. He should have known

Danny was a survivor, and that she would be every bit as tough this morning as she had been last night, when she had told him what he could do with his gifts and his money.

They saddled up in silence and rode out together. They didn't speak until they reached the river, where he dismounted.

Danny joined him. 'So?' she said.

'So,' he echoed, staring out across the river. 'When are you leaving?'

'Soon.'

He ground his jaw, but acknowledged this. 'This is not how I expected to spend the first day of my married life—but then I didn't expect to get married at all,' he admitted. 'My parents put me off marriage when I was a child, with their shouting and squabbling over what was left of my grandfather's money.'

'You were put off marriage until you were forced to marry. Isn't that it, Tiago?'

'Yes,' he admitted bluntly.

'Were you hunting for a bride at Lizzie's wedding, when I practically ran into you?'

'You were so angry and shocked—I seem to remember you almost knocked me over. You would probably have liked to, anyway. As for hunting for a bride... Yes, I did scan the pool for likely candidates, and you were close to the top of my list.'

'Only close?' Danny said dryly, staring out across the river.

'I judged you too vulnerable to be drawn into my plan.'

'And now, Tiago?' She swung around to face him, but there was no warmth in her eyes.

'I was wrong about you,' he admitted. 'I should have known you were strong enough to take up any challenge.'

'And more than willing,' she remembered, smiling faintly.

He made no comment.

'And then I made the mistake of falling in love with you. We got close so fast that even our crazy wedding made sense.'

'It wasn't so fast,' he argued, frowning. 'We were close in Brazil.'

'Friends,' she conceded. 'You liked teasing me.'

'Yes, I did. And, as I remember it, you liked it too.'

She shrugged, slanting him a smile, but refused to comment.

'My grandfather was delusional, Danny. Don't you think after the childhood I experienced I would want to do something better for my children? I certainly wouldn't risk any child of mine growing up thinking I'd *bought* it. And you...' He paused and looked at her steadily. 'You're a very special woman, and someone I'm proud to call my wife.'

'If you could pull out of our deal, though, would you?'

He frowned. 'This is no longer a deal, Danny.'

'But it still feels like one to me.'

'So what can I do to change that?'

'I don't know,' she said honestly. 'I've never wanted anything from you in the material sense, but it was part of the deal. Maybe I can't live with that. Maybe my problem is with me and my judgement, not you. My only thought was to secure my mother's future and buy my own establishment. I couldn't see further than that. I didn't once think about the true cost...'

'You wanted to spread your wings,' he argued hotly. 'There's nothing wrong with that, and you still can. You want to taste adventure? It's right here.'

He had thought he was getting through to her, but instead of moving towards him she moved back towards her horse and mounted up.

'I need more,' she said softly. 'I need to prove myself before I have anything to offer you.'

He opened his arms in a gesture of surrender. 'You're so wrong. You don't have to prove anything to me. But, please, keep the money. You're going to need it if you go. Take it for your mother—make her secure. Give yourself a future, Danny.'

'I wanted you,' she said. 'I wanted your love. I wanted a life together.'

'And you can have it.'

'But how can I be sure that there won't be another time when you hide something from me in the mistaken belief that you're protecting me?'

'You can't,' he said bluntly, resting his hand on the neck of her horse. 'I won't commit to a promise I'm not certain I can keep. If you need protecting I'm going to do that, whatever you have to say about it.'

He tensed as she turned her horse for home.

'So you're just going to give up? You're not even going to fight for us?'

'For *us*?' she said, gathering up her reins. 'There is no "us", Tiago. There never has been. And, as you say, I have a life to lead and so do you.'

'But I love you.'

Tiago loved her. But her own feelings were in turmoil. She owed it to both of them to sort herself out... Would this *ever* work out?

'At least think it through,' Tiago insisted. 'You don't have to go right away. You've been just as cut off from emotion as I have, but if the last half-hour is anything to go by we've unlocked something in each other. Don't throw that away, Danny.'

She'd hurt him and she didn't know how to make it right, Danny thought as Tiago brought his horse along-side hers. She blamed herself. She should never have agreed to such a cold-blooded agreement. It had never been going to turn out well. She should have been content to stay where she was, with her heart in one piece.

'Where will you go? What will you do?' he said.

'I'll go back to Scotland and get a job.'

'Your qualifications are excellent,' Tiago agreed, as if he thought it was a good idea—or was that her inse-curity talking again? 'With your experience it shouldn't be hard to find work. But don't settle for just anything.'

'Stop worrying about me, Tiago. My decisions aren't all flawed. I'll rebuild my life and move forward.'

'I have no doubt you will, but I can't see how going back to Rottingdean is moving forward.'

'Maybe you're right. But I'm never going backwards again.'

CHAPTER TWELVE

HE RODE OUT with his collar turned up against the persistent drizzle, his jaw tightly clenched at the prospect of returning to an empty house.

Why hadn't he filed a flight plan? Any day without Danny was a damp, drizzly day, and she had been gone for over a month. In all that time no one had asked him about his missing bride. No one had dared to question him.

He had dealt with the yawning gap in his life by working longer hours and playing more polo. He had made improvements to the ranch and that had made him even angrier, wondering if Danny would like what he'd done. What did anything matter now?

She would always matter.

His security team had reported that, preferring to stand on her own feet rather than return to her old job at Rottingdean, Danny was now working as a Jack of all trades at a local stable close by the house in Scotland where she had worked for Lizzie's family. He respected Danny's wish to find herself, to be her own person, but respect didn't mean he was giving up on their relationship.

Yes. *Relationship.* They might have been married for only five minutes, but the bond between them was stronger than any piece of paper they had signed to silence his grandfather's lawyers.

Reining in, he turned for home. If he cared so much about Danny why was he still here?

He piloted the jet, but even he couldn't make it fly faster. He swore viciously at the thought of the time he'd wasted. But they were both stubborn, and Danny was still locked in the past. He appreciated that she needed time, but when had he ever hesitated before when he'd cared about something as much as this? He should have told her every detail from the start. Then she would not only have known the facts, she would also have known how he intended to deal with them. Instead he had tried to protect her, when what Danny needed was love and respect—not coddling.

He touched down in Scotland and leapt into the four-wheel drive he'd hired. He didn't wait. He didn't rest. He didn't sleep. Anticipation at the thought of seeing Danny was all it took to keep him wide awake.

He drove straight from the airport to the farm where she was working. He might have guessed it would be in a remote glen. Was she going to hide away here for the rest of her life?

His heart gripped tight when he spotted her. He hadn't expected it to be so easy, but she was working with a young colt in an outdoor arena. He climbed out of the vehicle and stood watching. He smiled, noticing how much she had learned from his training methods. He felt good about that, though standing back like this was an acute type of torture. And it was no more than he deserved.

The rampaging polo player the press talked about— the man who collected women like fine wine, drank deep and moved on—was in love. He'd only had to see

Danny again to know how deeply he loved her. His life was meaningless without her. He'd missed her every waking hour, and had lain awake each night thinking about her.

There'd been gossip since they'd parted. He couldn't expect the press to ignore the facts. *'Marriage is not for Tiago Santos!'* one of the reporters for a red-top had crowed, no doubt rejoicing in his misery. Danny must have read that article. And, yes, their marriage was un-usual, but Danny wasn't just any bride—she was *his* bride. She was the only bride he could ever want. The only *woman* he would ever want.

He tensed as she stilled, and wondered if she'd sensed him. Whatever Danny liked to think, they were keenly tuned to each other. Did she know he'd come to find her?

She turned slowly and stared straight at him. The wealth of feeling inside him as their stares held was in-describable. He stood motionless, absorbing every detail of her as she turned back to the pony and, saying some-thing, stroked its ears. Leaving the arena, she closed the gate and walked towards him. With every step she took he grew more certain that they belonged together, and that he would do anything it took to make this right.

He slanted her a smile as she walked up to him. 'How are you?'

'Good.'

She was pale, he thought as she studied his face in-tently.

'How are you, Tiago?'

'I'm fine.'

She didn't sound fine, and instead of taking the single step that would bring her into his arms she remained a few paces back, staring at him as if she couldn't believe her eyes.

'What brings you to the Highlands?'

Her voice, with its soft Scottish burr, rolled over him like a familiar pleasure—one he'd missed more than he could say. He had never felt so alert or more aware of Danny, more *alive*.

'I'm visiting old friends.'

'Chico and Lizzie?' She frowned. 'I didn't realise there were any upcoming polo matches.'

'Do I need an excuse?'

'So you've come here to train with Chico?' she guessed, searching his face.

'I'm here to see *you*, Danny.'

She collected her breath quickly and exhaled raggedly. Her breath clouded in front of her face as they faced each other.

'I've stayed away for as long as I'm prepared to.'

'I thought we agreed—?'

'I didn't agree to anything,' he cut in. 'You left me. Remember? You wanted time to get your head together. I've given you time.'

'Are you here because of what they've started saying about us in the press?'

'Don't insult me.'

Biting her lip, she replied, 'They're saying our marriage was on the rocks before it began. But if you think I started that rumour—'

'I don't think that. And I'm not worried about what people think. Our marriage is our business. And, before you ask, no one can touch the ranch. The deeds are in my vault and that's where they will stay. So, you see, I am no longer in the market for a "convenient bride".'

She smiled a little, hearing her own words thrown back at her. 'So why are you here?'

'We've been apart long enough. Everyone on the ranch

misses you. Lizzie and Chico wonder why they don't see more of you. You've shut yourself away here. Lizzie misses you, Annie misses you—*Deus*, Danny, *I* miss you.'

He hadn't realised how much.

'Come back to us,' he said softly.

She remained silent and he looked around the run-down farm, with its broken fencing, peeling paintwork and neglected yard.

'I don't know what this proves. You must be working an eighteen-hour shift just to keep things on an even keel here.'

She firmed her jaw, but didn't deny anything he'd said.

'No one doubts you can stand on your own two feet, but why isolate yourself like this? Why are you punishing yourself, Danny?'

'I'm making a life,' she said simply. 'And I'm doing it without your money. I'm sure Lizzie understands why I must do this.'

'Lizzie might understand, but it doesn't stop her worrying about you. Is that fair? I don't understand you, Danny. I don't understand why you've separated yourself from people who care so much about you. I don't understand why you're pushing us all away.'

'You've no right to discuss me with Lizzie.'

'I've got every right. We care about you. Is that such an alien concept to you?'

'It is where you're concerned. I've never known you to express your feelings before.'

'And you're so open with *yours*?'

She turned, restless, uncertain, hovering, as if she wanted to go but also wanted to stay. 'Thank you for coming to see me,' she said at last. 'I do appreciate your concern—'

'For God's sake, Danny, I'm not the local doctor. I'm your *husband*.'

'Of one night,' she said. 'And I know this farm doesn't look much, but I enjoy my work here.'

'You'd enjoy any job with a horse attached to it. Is this a permanent position?'

Lifting her chin, she peeled off her riding gloves and blew onto her cold red hands. 'Nothing's permanent—is it, Tiago?'

Shaking his head, he ignored the jibe. At any other time he would have seized those hands and put them inside his jacket, so his blood could heat hers, but Danny was like an edgy colt that might bolt if he made any sudden movement.

Undaunted, he asked, 'How about lunch in town?'

She looked at him as if he were mad.

He shrugged. 'I'm hungry. It's nearly lunchtime. And it's far too cold to hold our reunion here.'

'But what would we have to talk about?'

He had to remind himself that he had vowed to take this slowly.

'I'm sure we'll think of something.'

The only possible reason she could come up with for sitting in the sedate hush of the Rottingdean tea rooms with a barbarian, whose face was coated in thick black stubble and whose brilliant smile made the elderly waitress primp and simper, was that it wasn't possible to ignore her husband when he was in town. Tiago had come all the way from Brazil, she reminded herself, and she owed him the common courtesy of a conversation—if only in the hope that they could find some sort of closure.

'Do you *have* to do that?' she demanded—an unreasonable demand, she registered a split second after the words left her mouth, as Tiago removed his jacket.

Just revealing the powerful spread of his shoulders was enough for her awareness of him to soar into the stratosphere. She would challenge anyone to spend the night with Tiago and then just blank it from their mind.

'You take it off, laddie,' one of the elderly waitresses advised, endorsing Danny's opinion that in this sun-starved land Tiago Santos was a rare treat. 'You'll never feel the benefit when you go outside if you don't take your jacket off,' she commented approvingly, and a dozen or so more women turned their heads to stare at the splendid sight of Tiago, whose powerful frame was clad in the finest black Scottish cashmere.

With a warm smile at the waitress, Tiago raised a brow as he turned to Danny.

'You wanted to hear about my place of work?' She judged that a safe enough topic to start off with.

'Go ahead.' Smiling faintly, he looked down as he attempted to ease his legs beneath the dainty table without sending it crashing to the floor.

'You're too big for here,' she said as she steadied the teapot.

'Too big for civilised company?'

She buried her face in her teacup.

'So?' he pressed with a faint strand of amusement in his voice when she failed to answer him. 'This farm where you're working…?'

'It's a tenancy,' Danny revealed, looking up now they were back on safe ground. 'The landlord lives off-site. He owns several similar properties, and he has asked if I would consider managing all of them for him.'

'Has he indeed?' Tiago's jaw tightened.

'There's no need to sound so suspicious. He's old

enough to be my grandfather and due to retire any time now. More tea?'

Tiago's eyes narrowed at her prim tone, drawing her attention to the fact that he was twice the size of any man in the tea room. His hair was thicker, blacker, wavier and more unruly. And you could take it as a flat-out fact that there wasn't another man in the place wearing a gold earring. Local skin was blue-white—freckled, in her case—while Tiago's skin was swarthy, and she was quite sure there wasn't a man in a fifty-mile radius who could boast anything close to his physique.

'I feel like a giant, trying to fit my frame into this chair.'

She was forced to smile when he eased his position gingerly. 'You'll break it if you move too suddenly,' she warned.

Dipping his head, he stared up at her in a way that sent heat to every part of her body. It was impossible to remain immune to Tiago's particular brand of charm, and impossible to forget how it felt to be held in his arms. And now every woman in the place was staring at him.

'I won't catch you if you fall,' she warned him when he tipped his chair back.

'You've already caught me, *chica*.'

Tiago's murmur and that black stare fixed onto hers made her think of one thing only—and it wasn't tea.

'Are you ready to go?' he said.

She was about to leave when the bell tinkled over the door and Hamish, the gamekeeper, and his crew walked in. She was glad of the distraction, and surprised when Hamish acknowledged Tiago as if they were old friends—but then she remembered that they would have met at Chico's.

'Are you okay, Danny?' Hamish asked gruffly.

'Yes. Thank you.'

After the two men had exchanged greetings, and Hamish had gone to find a table, Tiago turned to her. 'Come to dinner with me tonight.'

'I'm sorry?'

'You will be if you refuse me,' he threatened with a wicked smile.

She gave him a warning look that didn't deter him at all. 'Are you asking me out?'

'That's exactly what I'm doing,' Tiago confirmed.

His lips pressed down, drawing her attention to the fact that he was badly in need of a shave—as usual. Imagining that stubble scraping her skin was a breath-stealing reminder of how it had felt when he kissed her.

'It's harmless,' he said. 'We're married, and I'm in town.'

Nothing was harmless where Tiago was concerned, but she couldn't bring herself to let him go yet. 'I have to eat, and so do you. Why not?'

Why not? She could think of a thousand reasons why not. Discarding them all, she allowed her imagination to run riot for a moment... Screaming with pleasure in Tiago's arms would be preferable to sitting across a table from him...

'Danny?'

She pulled herself round fast and smiled into his eyes. 'So you're asking me out on a *date*?'

Tiago frowned slightly. 'I suppose I am.' But his eyes were dancing with laughter too.

It would be all right. She would confine herself to chatting about people they knew. She would keep the conversation, as well as everything else, on safe ground.

'Stop frowning, Danny. It's a meal and a catch-up, and then I'll take you home.'

Now she just had to convince herself that that was exactly what she wanted. 'That sounds good,' she agreed. 'Yes,' she said softly.

Tiago smiled his bad-boy smile. 'You *do* know that a candlelit dinner is usually a prelude to sex?'

'If you think that's going to tip the balance—' She stopped, noticing that the respectable townsfolk at the tables surrounding them were listening in with avid interest.

'I think they like me,' Tiago murmured, with amusement in his dark eyes.

She sucked in a sharp breath as he lifted her hand to his lips.

'Stop,' she warned him, pulling her hand back. 'I've agreed to supper—nothing more.'

'That's all I'm offering,' Tiago assured her. 'Sex isn't on the menu tonight.'

Now she was hit by doubt. *Why* didn't he want sex? Had Tiago found someone else? She felt sick at the thought.

'If this is another of your games…'

Leaning across the table until their faces almost touched, he whispered, 'The only game I play is polo.'

'Is it?' She was still tense.

'Although I do have a repertoire of games that don't require a horse and a mallet to make them fun.'

She made an incredulous sound as Tiago sat back with a confident smile on his face. He continued to regard her steadily, his amused black stare warming her, and even when he looked away to call for the bill a sweet pulse of desire throbbed deep inside her.

CHAPTER THIRTEEN

DANNY WAS ALWAYS CALM, always measured—at least that was what she told herself—except for tonight, when she was catapulting from one side of her room to the other, trying on clothes and trying to decide how she should wear her hair.

Finally she stood back, arms folded, wondering how it was possible for one person to buy so many sale rejects in the hope that one day she would find just the right accessory to pull the hopelessly mismatched set of items together. She had never pulled an outfit together in her life. She had always been a tomboy in jeans.

And she had around five minutes before Tiago was due to arrive to pick her up and take her to supper.

Why had she left things to the last minute?

She blamed it on the shortbread.

In the spirit of keeping things platonic, and to show Tiago some true Scottish hospitality, she had used her small worktop oven and her grandmother's secret recipe—sure to melt all but the stoniest heart—to bake him a tray of the traditional Scottish cookies, so he didn't think she was accompanying him tonight solely in the expectation of a free meal.

Tied up with a tartan ribbon, the small cellophane

packet was a humble offering, but it was the best she'd been able to come up with in the time available.

Tiago took a shower, shaved, and tamed his hair in as much as it could be tamed. He even put on a jacket and tie with his jeans for the occasion. He checked himself over in the mirror. He looked like an undertaker. Ruffling his hair, he ditched the tie, opened a couple of buttons at the neck of his shirt and tugged on a sweater. *Better.*

Danny was waiting for him in the biting cold outside her front door. Because she didn't want him to see where she lived, he suspected. The farm seemed even more dilapidated and unappealing to him on second viewing. He didn't like the thought of her living here on her own.

'You didn't have to wait out here.' He ushered her towards the four-wheel drive

'I didn't want to keep you waiting,' she said, standing back as he opened the door for her. 'Where are we going?'

'I can't say.'

'You can't say or you won't say?'

He smiled. 'You decide.'

'Maybe I won't come with you.'

'You'll come,' he said confidently. 'You never could resist an adventure.'

He would forgive her anything tonight. Just the fact that she had gone to some trouble with her appearance was enough for his groin to tighten with appreciation—though he would take her straight from mucking out a stable if he had to. Fortunately, that wasn't necessary. Her hair was shining and she was wearing the familiar wild-flower scent, and make-up—just a touch, but enough to suggest she wasn't completely switched off.

'You'd better not be teasing me with this supper,' she warned him, frowning in a way that made him want to grab her close and kiss her hard. 'You tell me where we're going or I'm not moving another step.'

Maybe the signs weren't *all* good, he amended, hiding his amusement. 'I'm taking you somewhere new.'

'Tiago,' she said patiently, 'there is nowhere new. This is the Highlands of Scotland, where nothing has changed for a thousand years.'

His lips curved with amusement, but he wouldn't be drawn. Strolling round to the driver's side, he got into the vehicle.

'Where *is* this?' Danny demanded a short time later, as he swung the wheel to turn the four-wheel drive onto a recently resurfaced driveway lined with majestic snow-frosted pines.

'You tell me. You've lived in Rottingdean all your life—where nothing ever changes,' he reminded her dryly.

'But this place has been derelict for years.' She frowned as she stared out of the window.

'Not any longer.'

'When did it become a hotel?'

'Never, as far as I'm aware.'

She turned ninety degrees to stare at him. 'What do you mean?'

'I live here. At least I'm planning to spend a good part of the year here.'

A stunned silence greeted this remark.

'I apologise if this comes as a shock to you, Danny, but as you haven't been talking to me lately...' He shrugged. 'It's better that you know. I can hardly be your neighbour and spend time at a house down the road without you noticing at some point.'

'Let me get this straight. Are you telling me that you've bought the Lochmaglen estate?'

'And the whisky distillery.'

'You're going into business here?' Danny's eyes widened.

'I like Scotch.'

'Tiago!'

'Lochmaglen will form part of my business empire, but I won't allow any investment to be a drain on my finances. Everything I put money into has to earn its keep.'

'Is that what you thought about me?' she asked him lightly.

'You sent the money back.'

'Yes, I did.' She sounded pleased about that.

Tiago continued without comment. 'I mostly bought this place for the excellent pasture—or it will be excellent once I've reclaimed it from the weeds. I'm going to build a new training facility for my horses.'

'But you've got excellent training facilities in Brazil.'

'On the other side of the world,' he pointed out. 'But now I'm setting up in Scotland—to service my European interests.'

This made perfect sense to him, but Danny was shaking her head.

'Don't think I'm coming to work for you. I'm very happy where I am.'

'Good,' he said flatly. 'You couldn't have said anything to please me more.'

Was that a flash of disappointment on her face?

'Ah, there's Annie!' he exclaimed as he stopped the vehicle at the foot of the steps leading up to the sturdy front door of the ancient manse.

Hamish's wife, Annie, the housekeeper at Rottingdean, had offered her services for the night, and was standing ready on the steps, waiting to welcome them.

'You leave no stone unturned, do you, Tiago?' Danny threw at him as she waved at Annie.

'No,' he admitted. 'Annie's missed you. It's time you two were brought together. So, what do you think I have in mind for tonight?'

She firmed her jaw and refused to answer.

'You do remember what *isn't* on the menu for tonight?'

'Sex,' she said, turning her cool stare on his amused face.

'That's right.' Tiago's mouth curved in a smile. 'Whatever you want, whatever you need—you're not going to get it tonight.'

'You are such an arrogant barbarian.'

'But you knew that from the start.'

'What makes you think—?'

'Danny, please...' He gave her a look and saw her eyes darken. 'We should go in. Annie's waiting to spoil you.'

'I don't need spoiling.'

'Don't you?' He reached across to open her door and paused. 'You've got shadows under your eyes. Have you been working all hours?'

'What's it to you?'

She turned away, shutting him out. He'd done his research and knew without her telling him that she was trying to shore up a failing stable on her own, with no financial input from the landlord whatsoever. Danny was too proud to take money from anyone—even when she'd earned it. She'd seen difficulty and hardship, and instead of turning her back had responded by throwing her heart and soul into the job. No wonder she looked so tired. She had to be exhausted.

'What are your hours?' he demanded as he helped her down from the four wheel drive

'Whatever's required,' she said.

He believed her.

'I'm building a nest egg. Remember that?'

'You're not going to build it at that place—there's not even the money to pay you a fair wage.'

She didn't answer this.

Taking hold of her hand, he helped her down. She let go of him at the first opportunity.

'I hope I'm dressed appropriately tonight?'

He smiled. She never could resist making a teasing barb. He took it as a good sign.

'You're dressed perfectly.'

However tired she was, Danny would always look beautiful to him. However limited her budget, she looked like a queen. Tonight, in a simple dress of moss-green wool, and a pair of shoes that—well, the best that could be said for them was that they weren't riding boots—she had a natural elegance that would put the society women he'd used to date to shame.

'Let's get one thing straight,' she said at the foot of the steps.

'By all means,' he said pleasantly.

'I only agreed to come to supper with you tonight because—'

'Because…?' He prompted with an amused stare.

'Because you're a stranger in town, and because it would be rude to ignore you.'

'Extremely rude, considering you're my wife,' he agreed. 'Come on. Let's not keep Annie waiting.'

Annie swept Danny into a hug, and then chivvied her up the steps and into the welcoming warmth beyond the sturdy front door.

'I've prepared you both a lovely supper and left it in the library, where you'll be snug,' the housekeeper was telling Danny breathlessly as she ushered them down the newly redecorated hall.

Tiago followed the two women into the library, glad to see them so close and Danny so happy. Asking Annie to come was a masterstroke. Danny had relaxed instantly in the older woman's company.

'This is a beautiful room,' she said, turning to him now.

'Thank you.'

He was very proud of the library. He had dreamed of a room like this—of the adventures contained within the covers of a book—ever since he was a child, and had created a library exactly to that dream design. He'd recoiled at his designer's suggestion that he buy books 'by the yard', and had handpicked each one and had them shipped to Scotland.

The room was perfection, in his eyes, and never more so than now, with a fire burning lustily in the hearth, a feast prepared by Annie spread out on the table, and the woman he loved standing in the centre of the room. gazing around with wonder at the walls filled with books.

Yes. He loved her—more than anything on this earth.

'I can't believe how stupid I was not to realise all this was going on down the road!'

'Not stupid,' he argued as Annie smiled and left them to it. 'My people are the best, and they were under strict instructions not to create any upheaval with their heavy vehicles in the village—and I didn't exactly run a banner across the sky.'

'But still,' she argued, running her hand across the newly refurbished mantelpiece. 'You've restored everything to its original state. This is wonderful, Tiago.'

'I'm glad you like it.'

He had wanted to bring the old place back to life again, and now Danny was standing here he felt he had succeeded. The library was large and airy, with French doors leading out onto the newly reformed gardens, and there was a large oak table in the centre of the room, where he could sit and spread out his papers, but it was Danny who held his attention now.

As she shook her head in surprise at one new discovery after another her hair caught the light and gleamed as if it were coated with gold dust. All the suspicion had gone from her face and all that was left was happiness. He could almost believe they had never been apart.

'What?' he asked as her head shot up and she turned round to look at him.

'I'm such a fool. I almost forgot.'

'Will you stop saying that? You are *not* a fool,' he insisted as she hurried back to the chair where she'd left her bag. Goodness knew what her mother had called her in the past, but he could imagine.

She delved inside her bag and rummaged around, before handing him a scrunched-up pack of biscuits. Taking care not to touch his hand, she said, 'I'm afraid they're a bit broken, but I made them for you. It's traditional Scottish shortbread. We hand it out to visitors to encourage them to come back.'

'Is that what you're doing now, Danny?'

Her cheeks flushed red as he stared into her eyes. Her gift thrilled him. He had been given a full-blood Arabian stallion by the daughter of a sheikh, and a watch beyond price by a princess—both of which he had returned. Well, he had bought the horse for a fair price later, at auction... But nothing in his life had meant more to him than this packet of broken biscuits.

Broken? They looked as if they had been pulverised between Danny's wringing hands.

'You *do* eat carbs?' she asked worriedly.

He raised an amused brow. 'Please...'

'Okay.' She risked a smile. 'Only some sportsmen—'

Danny had stopped talking, as if something in his face had made her think he was going to kiss her. It was sad to think his wife knew so little about him—but then they were both to blame for that.

'We should eat,' he said, moving away to give her space. 'Annie's made a feast for us. I'll show you round later, if you like?'

'I'd like...' Danny's brows drew together, as if she was trying to figure him out. 'If this library is anything to go by, I suspect you've worked wonders on the rest of the house.'

'You can judge for yourself after supper.'

She had seriously underestimated the effect of being close to Tiago after having spent so much time apart from him. When he didn't look at her, her heart thundered with disappointment. And when he did look at her she could hardly breathe. And through all this she was supposed to appear cool and detached...

It shouldn't be hard, when Tiago was so calm, but keeping her own counsel was proving almost impossible when she longed to ask him about so many things. Like what was left between them now Tiago no longer needed a wife?

Maybe the answer was in his manner. He was behaving more like an old friend keen to show her round his new house than a lover—let alone a husband. She would just have to adapt to this new situation between them, and fall into a similar role.

* * *

They took the tour after supper. He had to try very hard not to notice the soft dark green wool stretching over the plump swell of Danny's buttocks as she walked in front of him, or her nipples pressing against the soft fabric through the fine lace of her bra. He concentrated instead on his wife's animated face and the brilliance of her eyes, and relished the fact that it was thanks to Danny that he had learned so much about himself. He knew now that he wasn't wholly gaucho *or* playboy, but a man determined to do his best. And if that meant curbing his playboy ways…

'I like you here,' Danny murmured as she looked around his home. 'You seem more real.'

He laughed. 'Do you mean I'm a hologram in Brazil?'

'No. A barbarian,' she said without hesitation.

'Would you have me any other way?'

From the blush on her cheeks, he guessed not.

She started making thoughtful comments about the décor, but all he could think about was taking her to bed, pleasuring her through the night, and not even bothering to muffle her screams of pleasure.

Yes, he had aimed for discreet but sumptuous country casual, he agreed distractedly. And, yes again, he was glad she approved of the colour scheme. But frankly he wasn't interested in jewel colours and expensive art when he had a living, breathing work of art standing in front of him, waiting to be undressed.

'Nothing too obviously billionaire chic?'

He laughed at her comment. 'I suppose you could say that.'

'So, who did you use?'

He frowned. He knew whose *body* he'd like to use—right after he'd pleasured it into a state of erotic euphoria. 'No one.'

Her gaze dropped to his lips. 'You mean you designed this all by yourself?'

'All except the library. Would you like to see the rest of it?' He led the way to the stairs.

'Why not?'

CHAPTER FOURTEEN

TIAGO'S BEDROOM WAS full of mellow wood and rich coloured drapes—a necessity in the Highlands, where the wind could be cruel and even well-insulated houses could be gripped in a frozen chill for months on end. There were tasteful accessories in a variety of muted honey colours, and crisp white linen on the bed. Two elegant lamps stood one either side of the bed on nightstands covered in books.

Feeling him close behind her, she turned and almost collided with him. From the way he was looking at her it was as if he knew everything she had been thinking... dreaming. Gathering herself quickly, she ignored the glint of understanding, and, yes, even humour in his eyes.

'Are you ready to go home, Danny?'

The way he was prompting her didn't leave her with much option. He had even stood back to clear her way to the door.

'Thank you for showing me around.' She sketched a smile. She couldn't pretend she wasn't disappointed that the evening was over so soon, but what had she expected? 'You have a beautiful home,' she said truthfully. 'I wish you every happiness living here. And in Brazil too, of course.'

He escorted her to the door and helped her on with

her jacket. He'd been the perfect gentleman throughout the entire evening. She knew she shouldn't hope for anything more, but having Tiago back in her life, even in a new way, was disturbing…upsetting. He was a complex man who demanded life on his own terms—as she demanded life on *her* terms. How had she ever imagined they could meet in the middle?

They couldn't, she concluded as Tiago helped her into the car and closed the door.

Why had he bought a Scottish estate? It couldn't be Chico's influence. No one influenced Tiago. She could understand him falling in love with the Highlands. Who wouldn't? This rugged setting was a scenic feast and, as he'd said, this was a perfect base for him. But how would she feel with her estranged husband living down the road? What if he found someone else? What if Tiago had children with that person? Could she look on and feel nothing?

'Are you all right?' he asked, flashing a concerned glance at her after a long silence.

'Yes. Thank you.' If he had been trying to jolt her into feeling passionately about him—about life, about everything—he couldn't have planned this evening better. And now she couldn't resist asking him… 'How long do you think you'll spend here each year?'

'That all depends.'

She waited, but Tiago revealed nothing more. His attention was fixed on the icy road. How could they have become so distant? Had she really thought she could handle this? How wrong she'd been.

'We'll go riding on the estate tomorrow.'

Her head shot up, but then she remembered her job. 'I'm afraid I can't.'

'Your work?'

'Yes.'

'You can take time off. I've spoken to your employer.'

She frowned. 'You didn't think to ask me first?'

'Forgive me.'

Tiago was mocking her a little bit, but she would forgive him anything for one of those smiles.

'It was a spur-of-the-moment impulse,' he admitted.

'You can't just walk back into my life and take over.'

'Shall I see you to your front door?' he asked, unfazed by this.

'That's not necessary—'

Ignoring her, he came round anyway and helped her out of the car. His touch was electric. She pulled back, still annoyed at the thought of her employer's likely reaction when a world-famous polo player had knocked on his door, demanding that one of his staff have time off.

'Thank you very much for tonight,' she said formally, turning to face Tiago at the front door. 'But please don't interfere in the life I'm making here in future.'

Inclining his head in a way that might have meant yes, or no, he smiled. Taking the key from her hand, he opened the front door. She flinched when he took hold of her shoulders, and then softened beneath his touch. She couldn't help herself. Her reaction was automatic. The bond between them could survive anything, and nothing she could do or think would change that.

'Goodnight, Danny...' Dipping his head, Tiago brushed a chaste kiss against her cheek.

'Goodnight...'

Her stomach clenched with disappointment as he walked away.

He stood beneath a shower turned to ice, and then rubbed himself down roughly before falling naked into bed.

Cursing viciously, he punched the pillows. Turning this way and that, he felt like a frustrated wolf that would be better off howling at the moon.

He'd get no sleep tonight. Seeing Danny again had thrown him completely. He had thought he was ready for it—ready for *her*—and that the time for their reunion had come and he'd be able to handle it. Now he wasn't sure of anything—except that his love for her had grown. And he wanted her more than ever.

Every wasted second was a second too long. He was in the most acute agony of his life. Mental frustration and physical frustration had combined to torture him.

He turned restlessly as his cell phone pinged. Picking it up, he scanned the number, then closed it down. He would not talk to Danny tonight—not over the phone. Nothing but having her in bed beside him would do. They belonged together.

But he'd waited for her this long and he could wait a little longer. What was pain?

He rejoiced in her strength, and in the fact that she had built a life for herself here. He even, however begrudgingly, had to admit that she was doing very well without him. So whatever she wanted from him tonight would have to wait until tomorrow morning.

The air was blue by the time Danny had pulled the bed-covers up to her chin. How *dared* Tiago come back into her life and interfere?

Had he found someone else?

Why else would he be so distant with her?

Had he lost all feeling for her?

Clearly he had.

How dared he refuse to take her call? She had wanted to warn him off one last time.

She had wanted to hear his voice before falling asleep.

How dared he speak to her employer without her express permission?

She took out her frustration on the pillow.

And how was everyone on the ranch?

Why hadn't he told her? Did that mean she was never going to see them again?

She picked up the phone to call him again but it went straight to voicemail. Again!

Damn the man! She didn't need him anyway!

She didn't need anyone!

Burying her head between the pillows, as if Tiago might hear her noisy sobs of anger and frustration, failure, longing and loneliness all the way over at the big house at Lochmaglen, she dragged the jacket of her flannelette pyjamas a little closer and curled up tightly in a ball.

She must have fallen asleep almost immediately, but woke feeling as if she hadn't slept at all. She had been dreaming about Tiago all night, Danny realised groggily. She'd been telling him how glad she was that he was back. And then they'd made love. She would never forget that dream. Her body would never forget that dream. She would always remember Tiago kissing her as if they'd spent a lifetime apart, rather than a matter of weeks. And then, when they had been resting, she'd told him she loved him, and Tiago had said he loved her too.

Dreams!

And now she had work to do. But first she had to speak to her employer and reassure him that she wouldn't be taking any time off—contrary to whatever he might have been told by their new and forceful neighbour.

She showered and dressed, and then ate breakfast. With a piece of buttered toast clamped between her teeth she hurried over to the stable block, and soon she was immersed in the work she loved.

But not for long.

Hooves clattering across the cobblestones reminded her that Tiago still expected them to ride out together this morning.

And what Tiago wants, Tiago gets...

Not on her watch.

That thought couldn't stop her heart going crazy. Whatever she thought of him—or of herself, or of the way she had handled their relationship up to now—Tiago would always make her world a brighter place. Just more annoying, she reflected with amusement as he rode into the yard.

'Nice horse,' she commented mildly.

Colossal understatement. Tiago was riding a fancy stallion that must have cost a king's ransom, and he was leading an equally fine grey at his side.

'Good morning, Danny.'

His voice played her like a violin, reverberating all the way through her.

'I trust you slept well?'

As well as he had, apparently. He had dark circles under his eyes too.

'Very well, thank you,' she said primly, while her body went on a rampage of lust.

With his swarthy skin, his unshaven face, and a bandana barely keeping his wild black hair under control, Tiago looked like every woman's answer to lonely nights. His relaxed way of riding suggested the master of the sexual universe had arrived. He was dressed in jeans and boots, and a rugged black jacket with the collar turned up against the wind, but it was his dark eyes that held her.

This was ridiculous. She was in no mood for his nonsense this morning. Planting her hands on her hips, she confronted him. 'Have you forgotten that I told you I was working this morning?'

'I remembered.'

Dismounting, he secured both horses to a post, while she tried very hard not to notice the width of his shoulders, his lean frame... And she definitely refused to notice his tight butt, along with the familiar bulge in his jeans.

'I left a message for my employer to let him know I will be working as usual this morning,' she announced crisply.

'I know you did.'

'You know?'

Tiago turned to face her and his expression was distinctly amused.

It took her a moment, and then the penny finally dropped. *'You!'*

He shrugged. 'Had you forgotten that this farm belongs to the Lochmaglen estate? Don't look so horrified, Danny. I made a very generous offer. Your ex-employer had no difficulty accepting it.'

'So you've bought up everything in sight?'

'Not quite. Chico and Lizzie still own Rottingdean.'

'So between you and Chico you've bought up half the Highlands?' She shook her head. 'You're incredible!'

'Glad you think so,' Tiago observed wryly, utterly unfazed.

'This isn't funny, Tiago. You could have told me last night, but instead you chose to dangle me on the end of your line. I won't let that happen again.'

'Mount up,' he suggested calmly. 'We can discuss this on the ride. And don't pretend you can resist checking out such a fabulous horse.'

True. He'd caught her looking at the mare. 'You've got a damn cheek.'

'I'm still trialling her,' he said, ignoring this, 'and I'd like to know what you think. I value your opinion, Danny. Is that so strange? You *have* had the best training in the world, after all.'

'And you can stop mocking me, and smiling like that, right now.'

Narrowing her eyes, she'd made the mistake of meeting Tiago's dark stare to say this, and now it was impossible to look away. His eyes held far too many wicked messages—messages that her body was all too eager to receive.

Tearing herself away from that distraction, she checked the tack and mounted up. 'You could have told me all of this last night.'

'I never show my hand on a first date.'

'A first date?' she queried, bending to flick the latch on the gate with her crop. 'Is that what you'd call it?'

'What would *you* call it?'

'You don't want to know.'

Tiago shrugged and then followed her through. 'Shall we just enjoy the ride and find out where it takes us?' he suggested, closing the gate behind them.

'I would need to erase the past for that.'

Danny urged her horse into a relaxed canter, but as Tiago rode alongside all the hurt came welling back.

'I would need to forget that you persuaded me to marry you without telling me what was involved. I would have to blank out the fact that you arranged a wonderful evening for us last night at a house you forgot to tell me you owned. And you even drew Annie into it—'

'Stop.' Tiago shifted position in the saddle so he could stare directly at her. 'Annie was eager to be part of last night, and I thought you were eager to be there. You were obviously pleased to see Annie—and you were eager to marry me, I seem to recall.'

'I *was* eager,' Danny admitted. 'I was eager and stupid and gullible. But not now. I gave you my heart and my trust in Brazil, but that was before I woke up. And I thought you knew me better than to imagine I could ever, *ever* involve a child.'

'Danny—'

'No,' she flashed, and with a click of her tongue she urged the grey mare to gallop away from him.

He wasn't staying back this time. This time he gave chase. They rode neck and neck at a flat-out gallop across the purple heather before finally reining in on the riverbank.

'What do you think of her?' he asked.

Danny looked at him as if she couldn't believe he could change tack so easily.

'The horse?' he prompted.

'I know what you're talking about,' she assured him. 'The horse is great.'

'She's great—but we're not?' he suggested, raising a brow.

Danny's face reflected her conflicting emotions. 'You had to find a wife—any wife—and there I was.'

'Yes,' he admitted. 'But I fell in love with you.'

'You fell in love with me?' she said. Her mouth slanted. 'If you'd loved me you would have told me the truth.'

'Maybe I didn't know what love was, but you taught me. I married you for the worst of reasons, but *graças a Deus* I saved the ranch. I'll make no apologies for that. Do I love you now? God help me, yes. Now more than ever.'

Swinging his leg over the horse, he dismounted. Running up his stirrups, he turned to stare at her.

'Do I ask you to forgive me? No. There's nothing for you to forgive. I will always love you, and I have never lied to you—'

'Except by omission,' she interrupted.

He shrugged. 'If I'd told you everything last night you would have thought, *The playboy is back. He thinks he can buy up everything in sight, including me.* I didn't want you to think that, Danny. I wanted the chance to speak to you and win your trust. I wanted to ride with you, out here in the open, where we have nothing to lose and everything to gain. I wanted to see your face when you saw the new mare. I rebuilt the house with you in mind, and I chose everything in it for you. Maybe I was wrong to believe there were some things it was better for you not to know, but I did it out of the best of reasons. I wanted last night to be special, unthreatening. I wanted to give us another chance. I didn't want what I can buy getting in the way of our reunion.'

'Like this horse?' Dipping her head, she nuzzled her face against the mare's silky neck.

'I wanted us to start afresh—just you and me last night, and then a new start for us this morning.'

Danny didn't say anything for a long time as they watched their horses drink, and then she said, 'You look tired.'

'So do you. Bad night?'

She curbed a smile. 'I didn't sleep much,' she admitted. 'But we can't just erase the past and start again, Tiago.'

'Why not?' He mounted up.

'Because your plan is redundant. You own Fazenda Santos and you don't need a wife.'

'But I need *you*. And what if I have a new plan? One that includes you? I'm going to turn this estate around,

Danny. I'm going to base it on my success in Brazil. You can help me, if you like. Unless that's a problem for you?'

'I couldn't possibly work fast enough to meet *your* exacting standards,' she commented.

'Really?' He pretended surprise. 'I found you satisfactory in Brazil.'

'Satisfactory?' she exclaimed. 'Watch it! I might be transparent when it comes to horses, but—'

'Not just horses,' he said.

'I'm certainly not vulnerable where you're concerned.'

'I don't think you're vulnerable at all,' he argued. 'I think you're strong—though you're far too trusting.'

'Tell me about it,' she said. And then a new thought occurred to her and she frowned. 'If this is your way of asking for my resignation…?'

'Certainly not,' he assured her. 'I'm going to put you to work.'

She held up her hand. 'Not so fast. If I do stay on I should warn you I'm unlikely to agree with you on most things.'

'Should I act surprised?'

'I won't be easy to work with,' she warned him, mounting up.

'Now I *am* surprised,' he murmured dryly as they both turned for home.

On the brow of the hill overlooking the old house of Lochmaglen, they stopped and reined in. They could see broken fencing stretching for miles from there.

He turned to Danny and smiled. 'I've always loved a challenge, haven't you?'

CHAPTER FIFTEEN

'I'VE NOT BOUGHT this place to see it fail,' Tiago told her as their horses clattered into the yard.

'But casualties are unavoidable?' Danny suggested as she dismounted.

'I hope not, but I can't afford to be weak. Weakness destroyed my family and almost destroyed Fazenda Santos. My parents were like yours—weak and easily led. I could never live through that again. So if you think I'm hard, understand why.'

'And if I find it hard to trust, understand why,' she countered.

'I do,' he assured her wryly. 'But luckily my main interest in life is rescuing and rebuilding.'

She laughed. 'I remember.'

He turned serious. 'But sometimes it's the tender things that get trampled—which is where you come in.'

'Me?'

'You brought the human touch to the ranch. I want you to do the same here'

'So what exactly is the job you're offering me?'

'The hardest job of all—the job of being my wife,' Tiago said as he hefted the saddle off his horse. 'And not just in name only, or for a year, but for a lifetime.'

'As long as that?' she said.

She turned to look at him and their stares met and held, and then they both laughed. It had been a long time coming, but they were finally back to their tormenting best—in a way they hadn't been since those early days of their friendship on Chico's ranch.

And now Tiago was in hunting mode, his firm mouth curving.

'You need to accept that I love you,' he said. 'You need to understand that when you walked out I was hurting too.' His lips pressed down as he thought back. 'But maybe I needed that wake-up call. I certainly got one when I almost lost you.'

'And now?' she said.

Tiago shrugged. 'Now I just want to know if I'm wasting my time here. Has your life moved on?'

'Has yours?'

Neither of them answered. Maybe they didn't need to. They had entered the stillness and shade of the stable block, and made swift work of settling their horses.

'So I've still got a job?' Danny confirmed as they walked outside.

'Yes. Of course.'

They stopped walking. Tension was rising. Did she move closer, or did he? Closing her eyes, she inhaled deeply, glutting herself on the sweet tang of leather and hot, clean man.

'What are you doing?' he asked as she stood on tiptoe.

'I'm going to kiss you.'

'That's my job.'

'You're too slow. This is just something else you're going to have to get used to. Barbarian mates tend to be as fierce as each other.'

She kissed him.

Tiago didn't move. 'Are you always going to be so forceful with me?'

'Always,' she promised.

'Then we are going to have a very interesting life together, Senhora Santos.'

'I certainly hope so.'

'I've missed you, Danny...' He stared into her eyes.

'I've missed you too.'

'Let's never fight again.'

'Unless we're in bed?' she suggested.

Tiago laughed, his breath clouding with hers in the frigid air. 'I will always love you, always protect you, always care for you—for as long as you will allow me to. And I will always support you in anything you decide to do.'

'Stop.' Reaching up, she placed her fingers on his lips. 'In your position I would have done exactly the same. We're like two halves of the same coin.'

'What are you saying, Danny?'

'Is it wrong to have sex on a second date?'

Deus! I need a bed,' Tiago said huskily as he slammed her against the wall. 'Why is there never a bed when I need one?'

'Let me!' Danny insisted fiercely. 'Why do you always wear so many clothes?'

'It's winter?'

'Stop making excuses.'

She tugged at his shirt, exclaiming when she got down to hot, hard skin. She threw her head back and rubbed her body against him, purring deep in her throat like a contented kitten.

'Not here—not like this,' Tiago insisted, plucking reason from the air when it was lost to both of them. 'We've

waited too long for this, and I've no intention of break-
ing such a long fast in a tack room.'

'All right,' Danny agreed grudgingly. 'But be quick—'

Tiago strode across the yard with her in his arms, into
the house and up the stairs, without pausing. Reaching
the bedroom, he kicked the door shut behind them and
they fell on each other. Clothes flew left and right. Words
were unnecessary. When they were naked she was ready
to scramble up him, but Tiago held her still and brought
her in front of him.

'No,' he said, speaking softly and intently as he stared
into her face. 'This has to be special for you.'

Carrying her to the bed, he laid her down gently.
Stretching out his powerful length beside her, he brought
her into the circle of his arms and proceeded to give love-
making a new meaning.

Keeping her arms above her head in one fist, he maintained eye contact as he built her pleasure with strokes
and gentle teasing, until she was wild for him and it was
all she could do to keep still. She had never felt like this
before—so full of love, so abandoned, so free. Free to
trust, to give, and to receive as Tiago introduced her to
a new and extraordinary level of pleasure.

A groan escaped her as he stroked her buttocks, en-
couraging her to open her legs for him. And then, after
teasing her with just his tip, he allowed himself to catch
inside her, but then moved away again, making her sob
with frustration.

'More…'

'More?' he queried in a low, husky voice.

'Don't tease me,' she begged him. 'I've waited too
long for this.'

She gasped with relief when he allowed her another
exquisite inch.

But then he pulled back again.

'Are you trying to drive me crazy with frustration?'

'No. I'm making sure you trust me. Completely and for ever this time.'

He took her again, by a couple of inches, and then he rested, allowing her to savour how good it was. Then he began to move, slowly and steadily, thrusting his hips to a dependable rhythm that had her screaming his name within seconds.

'Again,' she gasped as the strongest of the pleasure waves rolled over her and subsided. 'I must have more—please...please...more...again...'

Her fingers dug into him as she fell a second time, even more strongly than the first.

'Again, and again, and again,' Tiago promised her as he worked steadily to bring her more pleasure.

And this time when she quietened he murmured her name against her mouth and told her that he loved her.

They rode out the next morning, after a night of no sleep, but neither of them was tired for some reason. Tiago glanced at Danny and smiled. Life was too precious to waste a moment sleeping. They had done more than make love last night—constantly and vigorously; they had reached a new understanding built on trust and the realisation that neither of them was perfect, but they were better together than they could ever be apart.

The horses seemed to sense their exhilaration and it was a fast ride out and an even faster ride back. The horses were keen to get to their oats and hay nets, while Danny and he couldn't wait to go back to bed.

They went about the business of settling the horses as thoroughly as they always did, but with a careful speed. They didn't speak—they didn't have to—but each time they brushed against each other in the confined space he knew they felt the same bolt of electricity.

'So what do you think of the grey?' he demanded as they strode briskly across the courtyard to the house.

'I'd keep her, if I were you.'

'Really?' he said, opening the door and standing back to let her in.

'Definitely—she's responsive and intelligent. What more could you want?'

'What are you saying, Danny?' There was laughter in his voice. 'Are we still talking about the horse?'

Dragging her close, he stared deep into her eyes.

'That didn't require an answer, by the way,' he said as he led her towards the stairs.

She was breathless by the time they reached the bedroom, and that had nothing to do with the speed at which she'd climbed the stairs. Catching hold of her, Tiago swung her round and eased her down gently onto the coverlet.

'Are you sore after our excesses? Do you need me to go easy on you?'

She smiled. 'What do you think?'

Grabbing hold of Tiago by the front of his shirt, she pulled him down beside her. He didn't lose eye contact for a moment as he tugged off his shirt and quickly unlatched the buckle on his belt.

'You're beautiful,' she said as he pulled off his jeans.

'And you're overdressed. No—let me,' Tiago insisted.

He undid each of her buttons slowly, and after unfastening the zipper on her jeans eased them down. Each brush of his fingertips was surely intentional; each pulse of pleasure was certainly real.

'Let me touch you,' he whispered, holding her gaze. 'Let me pleasure you, Danny.'

'Don't you always?'

Tiago's mouth curved, and she was already so very sensitive that she exclaimed with excitement the moment he touched her.

'Don't look away. I want you to look at me, Danny, and I'll tell you when—'

'Now!' she wailed, unable to hold on.

'Greedy.' He laughed as he held her in his arms and she convulsed with pleasure. 'We do have all day and all night,' he reminded her as he kissed her.

'Is that all?' she complained.

'Believe me—I'm here for as long as you want. And I have no complaints.' He swallowed the last of her satisfied groans in a kiss. 'We have a lot of time to make up.'

'For every night apart?' she suggested.

'And every night going forward,' Tiago said.

It was a long time later, when they were stretched out dozing, with their limbs entwined, that Tiago murmured something Danny wasn't sure she'd heard correctly.

'Say again?' she murmured groggily.

'I said I love you, Danny, and I want to spend the rest of my life with you—so will you marry me?'

'No can do,' she said sleepily.

'Why not?' Tiago prompted huskily.

'I'm already married…my husband wouldn't like it.'

'Would he approve of a blessing in the local kirk?'

She stirred, properly awake now. 'You're serious?'

'I'm absolutely serious. I was thinking we could have our blessing at Rottingdean, so everyone can share the day. That is what you wanted, isn't it?'

'Yes… Yes, of course is it. But I do have one condition.'

'Name it,' Tiago growled.

'We spend our entire honeymoon in bed.'

'I'm sure that can be arranged,' he agreed as he gathered her into his arms.

EPILOGUE

THE TINY CHAPEL in the Highland village of Rotting-dean was filled to capacity for the blessing of Danny and Tiago's marriage vows. Tiago had flown everyone who mattered over from Brazil, and had even persuaded Lizzie's mother to make an appearance—though she had scooted off to meet up with her toy-boy some time before the end of the ceremony.

That apart, he was determined nothing would stand in the way of Danny's happiness. He had left nothing to chance—even buying Danny a more 'job-appropriate' ring to jostle alongside the jewels he loved to lavish on her.

'I intend to work you very hard,' he murmured as he slipped the simple platinum band on to Danny's wedding ring finger.

'I love it,' she whispered, glancing at the ring and then meeting and sharing the humour in his eyes. 'And as for working me hard—both in and out of the bedroom—I wouldn't have it any other way. Though I may have to take some time off...'

'Why?'

'Shh...' she warned him as the minister began to address the congregation once more.

'Are you going to make me wait before you explain that comment?' Tiago demanded, with his usual force.

'Tiago, I am going to make you a daddy. Now, please be quiet.'

She had never seen Tiago so happy. He couldn't wait to tell everyone their news when they arrived at the hotel where they were holding their reception.

'So you tamed the playboy?' Lizzie commented, giving Danny a hug. 'And I couldn't be more thrilled that we're both expecting our babies in the same month.'

'Hello, you two!'

'Emma?'

Danny couldn't have been more surprised to see a chirpy young girl with the same bright red hair as Lizzie wearing a chambermaid's uniform.

But why was she surprised, when Lizzie's cousin Emma had always worked hard and had always loved working with people? Danny only had to think back to the garden parties the three of them had used to organise under Lizzie's grandmother's supervision, to raise money for local charities, to remember that. With her bubbly personality, Emma Fane would be an asset wherever she worked.

'No wonder you hardly recognised me,' Emma exclaimed, giving Danny an enthusiastic hug. 'It has been almost ten years since I last visited Rottingdean.'

Emma had been little more than a child then. 'Of course I recognise you...' Danny was still computing the information. 'But I thought you were at college...?'

'I was—hotel management,' Emma confirmed, 'but then this—'

She stroked her stomach lovingly, which caused Danny to exchange a fast concerned glance with Lizzie.

Emma was a lot younger than they were, and seemed too young to be having a baby.

'And now I need the money,' Emma admitted bluntly. 'But don't worry about me,' she added brightly. 'This job at the hotel is great experience, and I love it here. Lizzie told me about the vacancy for a chambermaid, and here I am.'

Emma opened her arms wide, as if embracing the world and everything in it, with the infectious *joie de vivre* Danny had always associated with the young girl.

'I hope you don't mind me crashing your blessing,' she went on, 'but I'm just about to finish my shift and I couldn't resist peeping in.'

'Of course I don't mind,' Danny insisted. 'You're more than welcome to join us.'

'Oh, no,' Emma protested. 'I couldn't do that.'

'Why not?' Danny frowned. 'I'll speak to the manager for you.'

'If you're sure…?' Emma's face lit up.

'I'm certain. It will be good to catch up. I had no idea you were married—'

Danny stopped—blanched—wanted to cut out her tongue. She knew immediately from the look on Emma's face and Lizzie's sudden tension that she'd said the entirely wrong thing.

'Sorry—I didn't mean to infer anything.'

'It's an easy mistake to make,' Emma insisted. 'But please don't be embarrassed—I'm not. I couldn't be happier.'

'That's obvious,' Danny said warmly. 'So the three of us are going to share this exciting trip into motherhood together? You *are* sticking around?' she confirmed with Emma.

Emma was just about to answer when Tiago strolled

up to introduce them to a man—presumably another polo player, from the look of him—who might safely be called intimidating if you were of a nervous disposition.

Thankfully, Danny was not. She was used to daunting men, she thought as she glanced at Tiago, but for some reason she clutched Emma's hand a little tighter. She felt protective towards the young girl—and not just because Tiago's timing was so badly off. The little she knew about Emma's family suggested there would be no support for the young girl there, and Emma must be barely out of college—if she had even finished college at all.

There was a mystery here, Danny suspected. Emma had been such a promising student, and so serious about her career.

'Don't look so worried,' Emma whispered discreetly, before pulling away to leave Danny to mingle with her guests. 'I'm a lot tougher than I look.'

She would have to be, Danny concluded with concern as she noticed the daunting polo player staring after Emma. A vivacious, pretty girl like Emma would always attract plenty of male attention.

She turned back to Tiago, who was waiting to introduce her.

'Danny, this is Lucas Marcelos—another reprobate on the polo circuit.'

'I'm very pleased to meet you, Lucas,' she said politely. 'Welcome to Scotland.'

Danny's heart plummeted when she noticed that Lucas's attention was still fixed on Emma—though he covered his distraction fast, turning to face Danny with a stare that was piercing in its intensity.

'Tiago warned me you were beautiful,' he said, 'but now I see he was understating the case.'

Lucas's voice was deep and accented, and for some

reason it sent shivers down Danny's spine. She was glad when Tiago moved to stand between them.

'You're a lucky man,' Lucas told Tiago. 'I don't know what you've done to deserve such a woman, but you should give me your secret.'

'I love her. It's as simple as that and as complicated,' Tiago admitted as he looped a protective arm around Danny's shoulders. 'And she keeps me in line.'

'Which you *like*?' Lucas sounded incredulous at this.

'Which I adore,' Tiago insisted, in a way no man in his right mind would choose to argue with. 'You should try it some day, Lucas—find out for yourself.'

'That, my friend, is never going to happen.'

'You'd be surprised,' Tiago murmured, turning back to Danny as Lucas strolled away.

'Wow!' Danny released her pent-up tension in a gust of relief. 'Was I just scorched by an overload of testosterone, or was that a hologram of a very angry and frustrated man?'

'That, *chica*, was a good friend of mine who has taken more hits from life than he should have done. But I don't want to talk about Lucas now. I want to concentrate on you—if you don't mind?'

'I don't mind at all.'

Danny shook off the feeling of unease Lucas had given her as Tiago drew her into the shadows, where they could be alone for a moment, but she did feel sorry for Lucas. To be alone was not an enviable position to be in. She just hoped Lucas wouldn't decide to take out his bitter energies on young Emma tonight—because Emma was also alone, and a good deal more defenceless than a successful polo player like Lucas Marcelos.

'Danny?'

She gazed up at her husband, rejoicing that they were

together. No one and nothing would ever part them again, and soon there would be a new addition to the Santos family.

'I love you with all my heart,' Tiago whispered against her mouth, kissing her tenderly and repeatedly. 'And I can't bear to share you with anyone. Is that terrible of me?'

'Not at all.' Standing on tiptoe, she kissed him back.

'And now we're going to be three—'

'Or four—who knows?' she teased him.

'You've made me very happy,' Tiago growled, staring deep into her eyes. 'And that was before you gave me the news of our baby.'

Danny's gaze dropped to the firm, sexy mouth of the man she loved. 'Did you say you had taken a suite at the hotel, so we could freshen up after the blessing if we needed to?'

'That's right. I have,' Tiago confirmed.

'I need to freshen up.' She looked at him.

'Strange,' Tiago murmured, brushing her mouth with his. 'So do I...'

* * * * *

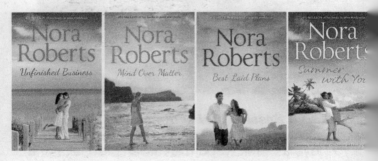

MILLS & BOON®

MODERN™

POWER, PASSION AND IRRESISTIBLE TEMPTATION

0415/01

Join our *EXCLUSIVE* eBook club

FROM JUST £1.99 A MONTH!

Never miss a book again with our hassle-free eBook subscription.

★ Pick how many titles you want from each series with our flexible subscription

★ Your titles are delivered to your device on the first of every month

★ Zero risk, zero obligation!

There really is nothing standing in the way of you and your favourite books!

**Start your eBook subscription today at
www.millsandboon.co.uk/subscribe**